STIFF UPPER LIP, JEEVES

Books by P. G. Wodehouse
available from Perennial Library

THE CAT-NAPPERS
HOW RIGHT YOU ARE, JEEVES
JEEVES AND THE FEUDAL SPIRIT
JEEVES IN THE MORNING
JEEVES AND THE TIE THAT BINDS
THE MATING SEASON
THANK YOU, JEEVES
THE WORLD OF JEEVES

P.G. WODEHOUSE

STIFF UPPER LIP,

PERENNIAL LIBRARY

Harper & Row, Publishers, New York
Grand Rapids, Philadelphia, St. Louis, San Francisco
London, Singapore, Sydney, Tokyo, Toronto

A hardcover edition of this book was published by Simon and Schuster in 1963.
It is here reprinted by arrangement.

First PERENNIAL LIBRARY edition published 1983. Reissued 1990.

Library of Congress Cataloging in Publication Data

Wodehouse, P. G. (Pelham Grenville), 1881-1975.
     Stiff upper lip, Jeeves.

     (Perennial library)
     Reprint. Originally published: New York : Simon and Schuster, 1963.
     I. Title.
[PR6045.O53S8 1983]   823'.912   83-47592
ISBN 0-06-097284-X

90 91 92 93 94   M PC 10 9 8 7 6 5 4 3 2 1

To
DAVID JASEN

CHAPTER
ONE

I MARMALADED a slice of toast with something of a flourish, and I don't suppose I have ever come much closer to saying "Tra-la-la" as I did the lathering, for I was feeling in mid-season form this morning. God, as I once heard Jeeves put it, was in His heaven and all right with the world. (He added, I remember, some guff about larks and snails, but that is a side issue and need not detain us.)

It is no secret in the circles in which he moves that Bertram Wooster, though as glamorous as one could wish when night has fallen and the revels get under way, is seldom a ball of fire at the breakfast table. Confronted with the eggs and b., he tends to pick cautiously at them, as if afraid they may leap from the plate and snap at him. List-less about sums it up. Not much bounce to the ounce.

But today vastly different conditions had prevailed. All had been verve, if that's the word I want, and animation. Well, when I tell you that after sailing through a couple of sausages like a tiger of the jungle tucking into its luncheon coolie I was now, as indicated, about to tackle the toast and marmalade, I fancy I need say no more.

The reason for this improved outlook on the proteins and carbohydrates is not far to seek. Jeeves was back, earning his weekly envelope once more at the old stand. Her butler having come down with an ailment of some sort, my Aunt Dahlia, my good and deserving aunt, had borrowed him for a house party she was throwing at Brinkley Court, her Worcestershire residence, and he had been away for more than a week. Jeeves, of course, is a gentleman's gentleman, not a butler, but if the call comes, he can buttle with the best of them. It's in the blood. His Uncle Charlie is a butler, and no doubt he has picked up many a hint on technique from him.

He came in a little later to remove the debris, and I asked him if he had had a good time at Brinkley.

"Extremely pleasant, thank you, sir."

"More than I had in your absence. I felt like a child of tender years deprived of its Nannie. If you don't mind me calling you a Nannie."

"Not at all, sir."

Though, as a matter of fact, I was giving myself a slight edge, putting it that way. My Aunt Agatha, the one who eats broken bottles and turns into a werewolf at the time of the full moon, generally refers to Jeeves as my keeper.

"Yes, I missed you sorely, and had no heart for whooping it up with the lads at the Drones. From sport to sport they . . . how does that gag go?"

"Sir?"

"I heard you pull it once with reference to Freddie Widgeon, when one of his girls had given him the bird. Something about hurrying."

"Ah yes, sir. 'From sport to sport they hurry me, to stifle my regret—'"

"'And when they win a smile from me, they think that I forget.' That was it. Not your own, by any chance?"

"No, sir. An old English drawing-room ballad."

"Oh? Well, that's how it was with me. But tell me all about Brinkley. How was Aunt Dahlia?"

"Mrs. Travers appeared to be in her customary robust health, sir."

"And how did the party go off?"

"Reasonably satisfactorily, sir."

"Only reasonably?"

"The demeanor of Mr. Travers cast something of a gloom on the proceedings. He was low-spirited."

"He always is when Aunt Dahlia fills the house with guests. I've known even a single foreign substance in the woodwork to make him drain the bitter cup."

"Very true, sir, but on this occasion I think his despondency was due principally to the presence of Sir Watkyn Bassett."

"You don't mean that old crumb was there?" I said, Great-Scott-ing, for I knew that if there is one man for whose insides my Uncle Tom has the most vivid distaste, it is this Bassett. "You astound me, Jeeves."

"I, too, must confess to a certain surprise at seeing the gentleman at Brinkley Court, but no doubt Mrs. Travers felt it incumbent upon her to return his hospitality. You will recollect that Sir Watkyn recently entertained Mrs. Travers and yourself at Totleigh Towers."

I winced. Intending, I presumed, merely to refresh my

[11]

memory, he had touched an exposed nerve. There was some cold coffee left in the pot, and I took a sip to restore my equanimity.

"The word 'entertained' is not well chosen, Jeeves. If locking a fellow in his bedroom, as near as a toucher with gyves upon his wrists, and stationing the local police force on the lawn below to insure that he doesn't nip out of the window at the end of a knotted sheet is your idea of entertaining, it isn't mine, not by a jugful."

I don't know how well up you are in the Wooster archives, but if you have dipped into them to any extent, you will probably recall the sinister affair of Sir Watkyn Bassett and my visit to his Gloucestershire home. He and my Uncle Tom are rival collectors of what are known as objets d'art, and on one occasion he pinched a silver cow creamer, as the revolting things are called, from the relation by marriage, and Aunt Dahlia and self went to Totleigh to pinch it back, an enterprise which, though crowned with success, as the expression is, so nearly landed me in the jug that when reminded of that house of horror I still quiver like an aspen, if aspens are the things I'm thinking of.

"Do you ever have nightmares, Jeeves?" I asked, having got through with my bit of wincing.

"Not frequently, sir."

"Nor me. But when I do, the setup is always the same. I am back at Totleigh Towers with Sir W. Bassett, his daughter Madeline, Roderick Spode, Stiffy Byng, Gussie Fink-Nottle, and the dog Bartholomew, all doing their stuff, and I wake, if you will pardon the expression so soon after breakfast, sweating at every pore. Those were the times that . . . what, Jeeves?"

"Tried men's souls, sir."

"They certainly did—in spades. Sir Watkyn Bassett, eh?"

[12]

I said thoughtfully. "No wonder Uncle Tom mourned and would not be comforted. In his position I'd have been low-spirited myself. Who else were among those present?"

"Miss Bassett, sir, Miss Byng, Miss Byng's dog, and Mr. Fink-Nottle."

"Gosh! Practically the whole Totleigh Towers gang. Not Spode?"

"No, sir. Apparently no invitation had been extended to his lordship."

"His what?"

"Mr. Spode, if you recall, recently succeeded to the title of Lord Sidcup."

"So he did. I'd forgotten. But Sidcup or no Sidcup, to me he will always be Spode. There's a bad guy, Jeeves."

"Certainly a somewhat forceful personality, sir."

"I wouldn't want him in my orbit again."

"I can readily understand it, sir."

"Nor would I willingly foregather with Sir Watkyn Bassett, Madeline Bassett, Stiffy Byng, and Bartholomew. I don't mind Gussie. He looks like a fish and keeps newts in a glass tank in his bedroom, but one condones that sort of thing in an old schoolfellow, just as one condones in an old Oxford friend such as the Rev. H. P. Pinker the habit of tripping over his feet and upsetting things. How was Gussie? Pretty bobbish?"

"No, sir. Mr. Fink-Nottle, too, seemed to me low-spirited."

"Perhaps one of his newts had got tonsillitis or something."

"It is conceivable, sir."

"You've never kept newts, have you?"

"No, sir."

"Nor have I. Nor, to the best of my knowledge, have

Einstein, Jack Dempsey, and the Archbishop of Canterbury, to name but three others. Yet Gussie revels in their society and is never happier than when curled up with them. It takes all sorts to make a world, Jeeves."

"It does, indeed, sir. Will you be lunching in?"

"No, I've a date at the Ritz," I said, and went off to climb into the outer crust of the English gentleman.

As I dressed, my thoughts returned to the Bassetts, and I was still wondering why on earth Aunt Dahlia had allowed the pure air of Brinkley Court to be polluted by Sir Watkyn and associates when the telephone rang and I went into the hall to answer it.

"Bertie?"

"Oh, hullo, Aunt Dahlia."

There had been no mistaking that loved voice. As always when we converse on the telephone, it had nearly fractured my eardrum. This aunt was at one time a prominent figure in hunting circles, and when in the saddle, so I'm told, could make herself heard not only in the field or meadow where she happened to be but in several adjoining counties. Retired now from active fox chivying, she still tends to address a nephew in the tone of voice previously reserved for rebuking hounds for taking time off to chase rabbits.

"So you're up and about, are you?" she boomed. "I thought you'd be in bed, snoring your head off."

"It is a little unusual for me to be in circulation at this hour," I agreed, "but I rose today with the lark and, I think, the snail. Jeeves!"

"Sir?"

"Didn't you tell me once that snails were early risers?"

"Yes, sir. The poet Browning in his *Pippa Passes,* having established that the hour is seven A.M., goes on to say, 'The lark's on the wing, the snail's on the thorn.' "

"Thank you, Jeeves. I was right, Aunt Dahlia. When I

slid from between the sheets, the lark was on the wing, the snail on the thorn."

"What the devil are you babbling about?"

"Don't ask me; ask the poet Browning. I was merely apprising you that I was up betimes. I thought it was the least I could do to celebrate Jeeves' return."

"He got back all right, did he?"

"Looking bronzed and fit."

"He was in rare form here. Bassett was terrifically impressed."

I was glad to have this opportunity of solving the puzzle which had been perplexing me.

"Now there," I said, "you have touched on something I'd very much like to have information *re*. What on earth made you invite Pop Bassett to Brinkley?"

"I did it for the wife and kiddies."

I eh-what-ed. "You wouldn't care to amplify that?" I said. "It got past me to some extent."

"For Tom's sake, I mean," she replied with a hearty laugh that rocked me to my foundations. "Tom's been feeling rather low of late because of what he calls iniquitous taxation. You know how he hates to give up."

I did, indeed. If Uncle Tom had his way, the revenue authorities wouldn't get so much as a glimpse of his money.

"Well, I thought having to fraternize with Bassett would take his mind off it—show him that there are worse things in this world than income tax. Our doctor here gave me the idea. He was telling me about a thing called Hodgkin's disease that you cure by giving the patient arsenic. The principle's the same. That Bassett really is the limit. When I see you, I'll tell you the story of the black amber statuette. It's a thing he's just bought for his collection. He was showing it to Tom when he was here, gloating over it. Tom suffered agonies, poor old buzzard."

"Jeeves told me he was low-spirited."

"So would you be, if you were a collector and another collector you particularly disliked had got hold of a thing you'd have given your eyeteeth to have in your own collection."

"I see what you mean," I said, marveling, as I had often done before, that Uncle Tom could attach so much value to objects which I personally would have preferred not to be found dead in a ditch with. The cow creamer I mentioned earlier was one of them, being a milk jug shaped like a cow, of all ghastly ideas. I have always maintained fearlessly that the spiritual home of all these fellows who collect things is a padded cell in a loony bin.

"It gave Tom the worst attack of indigestion he's had since he was last lured into eating lobster. And talking of indigestion, I'm coming up to London for the day the day after tomorrow and shall require you to give me lunch."

I assured her that that should be attended to, and after the exchange of a few more civilities she rang off.

"That was Aunt Dahlia, Jeeves," I said, coming away from the machine.

"Yes, sir, I fancied I recognized Mrs. Travers' voice."

"She wants me to give her lunch the day after tomorrow. I think we'd better have it here. She's not keen on restaurant cooking."

"Very good, sir."

"What's this black amber statuette thing she was talking about?"

"It is a somewhat long story, sir."

"Then don't tell me now. If I don't rush, I shall be late for my date."

I reached for the umbrella and hat and was heading for the open spaces when I heard Jeeves give that soft cough of his and, turning, saw that a shadow was about to fall on what had been a day of joyous reunion. In the eye which he was fixing on me I detected the auntlike gleam which always means that he disapproves of something, and when he said in a soupy tone of voice "Pardon me, sir, but are you proposing to enter the Ritz Hotel in that hat?" I knew that the time had come when Bertram must show that iron resolution of his which has been so widely publicized.

In the matter of head-joy Jeeves is not in tune with modern progressive thought, his attitude being best described, perhaps, as hidebound, and right from the start I had been asking myself what his reaction would be to the blue Alpine hat with the pink feather in it which I had purchased in his absence. Now I knew. I could see at a g. that he wanted no piece of it and that the picture rising before his eyes of the young master parading London's West End with it perched on his bean was plainly one that he viewed with concern and looked askance at.

I, in sharp contradistinction, was all for this Alpine lid. With me, when I saw it in the shop, it had been a case of love at first sight. I was prepared to concede that it would have been more suitable for rural wear, but against this had to be set the fact that it unquestionably lent a diablerie to my appearance, and mine is an appearance that needs all the diablerie it can get. In my voice, therefore, as I replied, there was a touch of steel.

"Yes, Jeeves, I am."

"Very good, sir."

"You don't like this hat?"

"No, sir."

"Well, I do," I said rather cleverly, and went out with it tilted just that merest shade over the left eyebrow which makes all the difference.

CHAPTER
TWO

My DATE at the Ritz was with Emerald Stoker, younger offspring of that pirate of the Spanish Main, old Pop Stoker, the character who once kidnapped me on board his yacht with a view to making me marry his elder daughter Pauline. Long story, I won't go into it now, merely saying that the old fathead had got entirely the wrong angle on the relations between his ewe lamb and myself, we being just good friends, as the expression is. Fortunately it all ended happily, with the popsy linked in matrimony with Marmaduke, Lord Chuffnell, an ancient buddy of mine, and we're still good friends. I put in an occasional weekend with her and Chuffy, and when she comes to London on a shopping binge or whatever it may be, I see to it that she gets her calories. Quite natural, then, that when her sister Emerald came over from America to study painting at the Slade, she should have asked me to keep an eye on her and give her lunch from time to time. Kindly old Bertram, the family friend.

I was a bit late, as I had foreshadowed, in getting to the tryst, and she was already there when I arrived. It struck me, as it did every time I saw her, how strange it is that members of a family can be so unlike each other—how different in appearance, I mean, Member A so often is from Member B, and for the matter of that Member B from Member C, if you follow what I'm driving at. Take the Stoker troupe, for instance. To look at them, you'd never have guessed they were united by ties of blood. Old Stoker resembled one of those fellows who play bit parts in gangster pictures; Pauline was of a beauty so radiant that strong men whistled after her in the street; while Emerald, in sharp contradistinction, was just ordinary, no different from a million other nice girls, except perhaps for a touch of the Pekingese about the nose and eyes and more freckles than you usually see.

I always enjoyed putting on the nose bag with her, for there was a sort of motherliness about her which I found restful. She was one of those soothing, sympathetic girls you can take your troubles to, confident of having your hand held and your head patted. I was still a bit ruffled about Jeeves and the Alpine hat and of course told her all about it, and nothing could have been in better taste than her attitude. She said it sounded as if Jeeves must be something like her father—she had never met him—Jeeves, I mean, not her father, whom of course she had met frequently—and she told me I had been quite right in displaying the velvet hand in the iron glove, or rather the other way around, isn't it, because it never did to let oneself be bossed. Her father, she said, always tried to boss everybody, and in her opinion one of these days some haughty spirit was going to haul off and poke him in the nose—which, she said, and I agreed with her, would do him all the good in the world.

I was so grateful for these kind words that I asked her if she would care to come to the theater on the following night, I knowing where I could get hold of a couple of tickets for a well-spoken-of musical, but she said she couldn't make it.

"I'm going down to the country this afternoon to stay with some people. I'm taking the four o'clock train at Paddington."

"Going to be there long?"

"About a month."

"At the same place all the time?"

"Of course."

She spoke lightly, but I found myself eyeing her with a certain respect. Myself, I've never found a host and hostess who could stick my presence for more than about a week. Indeed, long before that as a general rule the conversation at the dinner table is apt to turn on the subject of how good the train service to London is, those present obviously hoping wistfully that Bertram will avail himself of it. Not to mention the timetables left in your room with a large cross against the two thirty-five and the legend "Excellent train. Highly recommended."

"Their name's Bassett." I started visibly. "They live in Gloucestershire." I started visibly. "Their house is called—"

"Totleigh Towers?"

She started visibly, making three visible starts in all.

"Oh, do you know them? Well, that's fine. You can tell me about them."

This surprised me somewhat.

"Why, don't *you* know them?"

"I've only met Miss Bassett. What are the rest of them like?"

It was a subject on which I was a well-informed source, but I hesitated for a moment, asking myself if I ought to reveal to this frail girl what she was letting herself in for. Then I decided that the truth must be told and nothing held back. Cruel to hide the facts from her and allow her to go off to Totleigh Towers unprepared.

"The inmates of the leper colony under advisement," I said, "consist of Sir Watkyn Bassett, his daughter Madeline, his niece Stephanie Byng, a chap named Spode who recently took to calling himself Lord Sidcup, and Stiffy Byng's Aberdeen terrier Bartholomew, the last of whom you would do well to watch closely if he gets anywhere near your ankles, for he biteth like a serpent and stingeth like an adder. So you've met Madeline Bassett? What did you think of her?"

She seemed to weigh this. A moment or two passed before she surfaced again. When she spoke, it was with a spot of wariness in her voice.

"Is she a great friend of yours?"

"Far from it."

"Well, she struck me as a drip."

"She is a drip."

"Of course, she's very pretty. You have to hand her that."

I shook the loaf.

"Looks are not everything. I admit that any red-blooded sultan or pasha, if offered the opportunity of adding M. Bassett to the personnel of his harem, would jump to it without hesitation, but he would regret his impulsiveness before the end of the first week. She's one of those soppy girls, riddled from head to foot with whimsy. She holds the view that the stars are God's daisy chain, that rabbits are gnomes

[21]

in attendance on the Fairy Queen, and that every time a fairy blows its wee nose a baby is born, which, as we know, is not the case. She's a drooper."

"Yes, that's how she seemed to me. Rather like one of the love-sick maidens in *Patience*."

"Eh?"

"*Patience*. Gilbert and Sullivan. Haven't you ever seen it?"

"Oh yes, now I recollect. My Aunt Agatha made me take her son Thos to it once. Not at all a bad little show, I thought, though a bit highbrow. We now come to Sir Watkyn Bassett, Madeline's father."

"Yes, she mentioned her father."

"And well she might."

"What's he like?"

"One of those horrors from outer space. It may seem a hard thing to say of any man, but I would rank Sir Watkyn Bassett as an even bigger stinker than your father."

"Would you call Father a stinker?"

"Not to his face, perhaps."

"He thinks you're crazy."

"Bless his old heart."

"And you can't say he's wrong. Anyway, he's not so bad, if you rub him the right way."

"Very possibly, but if you think a busy man like myself has time to go rubbing your father, either with or against the grain, you are greatly mistaken. The word 'stinker,' by the way, reminds me that there is one redeeming aspect of life at Totleigh Towers—the presence in the neighboring village of the Rev. H. P. ('Stinker') Pinker, the local curate. You'll like him. He used to play football for England. But watch out for Spode. He's about eight feet high and has the sort of eye that can open an oyster at sixty paces. Take a line through gorillas you have met, and you will get the idea."

"You do seem to have some nice friends."

"No friends of mine. Though I'm fond of young Stiffy and am always prepared to clasp her to my bosom, provided she doesn't start something. But then she always does start something. I think that completes the roster. Oh no, Gussie. I was forgetting Gussie."

"Who's he?"

"Fellow I've known for years and years. He's engaged to Madeline Bassett. Chap named Gussie Fink-Nottle."

She uttered a sharp squeak.

"Does he wear horn-rimmed glasses?"

"Yes."

"And keep newts?"

"In great profusion. Why, do you know him?"

"I've met him. We met at a studio party."

"I didn't know he ever went to studio parties."

"He went to this one, and we talked most of the evening. I thought he was a lamb."

"You mean a fish."

"I don't mean a fish."

"He looks like a fish."

"He does not look like a fish."

"Well, have it your own way," I said tolerantly, knowing it was futile to attempt to reason with a girl who had spent an evening vis-à-vis Gussie Fink-Nottle and didn't think he looked like a fish. "So there you are, that's Totleigh Towers. Wild horses wouldn't drag me there, not that I suppose they would ever try, but you'll probably have a good enough time," I said, for I didn't wish to depress her unduly. "It's a beautiful place, and it isn't as if you were going there to pinch a cow creamer."

"To what a what?"

"Nothing, nothing. I was just thinking of something," I said, and turned the conv. to other topics.

She gave me the impression, when we parted, of being a bit pensive, which I could well understand, and I wasn't feeling too unpensive myself. There's a touch of the superstitious in my makeup, and the way the Bassett ménage seemed to be raising its ugly head, if you know what I mean, struck me as sinister. I had a . . . what's the word? . . . begins with a p . . . pre-something . . . presentiment, that's the baby . . . I had a presentiment that I was being tipped off by my guardian angel that Totleigh Towers was trying to come back into my life and that I would be well advised to watch my step and keep an eye skinned.

It was consequently a thoughtful Bertram Wooster who half an hour later sat toying with a stoup of malvoisie in the smoking room of the Drones Club. To the overtures of fellow members who wanted to hurry me from sport to sport I turned a deaf ear, for I wished to brood. And I was trying to tell myself that all this Totleigh Towers business was purely coincidental and meant nothing, when the smoking-room waiter slid up and informed me that a gentleman stood without, asking to have a speech with me. A clerical gentleman named Pinker, he said, and I gave another of my visible starts, the presentiment stronger on the wing than ever.

It wasn't that I had any objection to the sainted Pinker. I loved him like a b. We were up at Oxford together, and our relations have always been on strictly David and Jonathan lines. But, while technically not a resident of Totleigh Towers, he helped the Vicar vet the souls of the local yokels in the adjoining village of Totleigh-in-the-Wold, and that was near enough to it to make this sudden popping up of his deepen the apprehension I was feeling. It seemed to me that it only needed Sir Watkyn Bassett, Madeline Bassett, Roderick Spode, and the dog Bartholomew to saunter in, arm in arm, and I would have a full hand. My respect for my guardian angel's astuteness hit a new high. A gloomy bird, with a marked disposition to take the dark view and make one's flesh creep, but there was no gainsaying that he knew his stuff.

"Bung him in," I said dully, and in due season the Rev. H. P. Pinker lumbered across the threshold and, advancing with outstretched hand, tripped over his feet and upset a small table, his almost invariable practice when moving from spot to spot in any room where there's furniture.

CHAPTER
THREE

WHICH WAS ODD, when you came to think of it, because after representing his University for four years and his country for six on the football field, he still turns out for the Harlequins when he can get a Saturday off from saving souls, and when footballing is as steady on his pins as a hart or roe or whatever the animals are that don't trip over their feet and upset things. I've seen him a couple of times in the arena and was profoundly impressed by his virtuosity. Rugby football is more or less a sealed book to me, I never having gone in for it, but even I could see that he was good. The lissomeness with which he moved hither and thither was most impressive, as was his homicidal ardor when doing what I believe is called tackling. Like the Canadian Mounted Police, he always got his man, and when he did so the air was vibrant with the excited cries of morticians in the audience making bids for the body.

He's engaged to be married to Stiffy Byng, and his long years of football should prove an excellent preparation for setting up house with her. The way I look at it is that when a fellow has had plug-uglies in cleated boots doing a Shuffle-off-to-Buffalo on his face Saturday after Saturday since he was a slip of a boy, he must get to fear nothing, not even marriage with a girl like Stiffy, who from early childhood has seldom let the sun go down without starting some loony enterprise calculated to bleach the hair of one and all.

There was plenty and to spare of the Rev. H. P. Pinker. Even as a boy, I imagine, he must have burst seams and broken try-your-weight machines, and grown to man's estate he might have been Roderick Spode's twin brother. Purely in the matter of thews, sinews, and tonnage, I mean of course, for whereas Roderick Spode went about seeking whom he might devour and was a consistent menace to pedestrians and traffic, Stinker, though no doubt a fiend in human shape when assisting the Harlequins Rugby football club to dismember some rival troop of athletes, was in private life a gentle soul with whom a child could have played. In fact, I once saw a child doing so.

Usually when you meet this man of God, you find him beaming. I believe his merry smile is one of the sights of Totleigh-in-the-Wold, as it was of Magdalen College, Oxford, when we were up there together. But now I seemed to note in his aspect a certain gravity, as if he had just discovered schism in his flock or found a couple of choir boys smoking reefers in the churchyard. He gave me the impression of a two-hundred-pound curate with something on his mind besides his hair. Upsetting another table, he took a seat and said he was glad he had caught me.

"I thought I'd find you at the Drones."

"You have," I assured him. "What brings you to the metrop?"

"I came up for a Harlequins committee meeting."

"And how were they all?"

"Oh, fine."

"That's good. I've been worrying myself sick about the Harlequins committee. Well, how have you been keeping, Stinker?"

"I've been all right."

"Are you free for dinner?"

"Sorry, I've got to get back to Totleigh."

"Too bad. Jeeves tells me Sir Watkyn and Madeline and Stiffy have been staying with my aunt at Brinkley."

"Yes."

"Have they returned?"

"Yes."

"And how's Stiffy?"

"Oh, fine."

"And Bartholomew?"

"Oh, fine."

"And your parishioners? Going strong, I trust?"

"Oh yes, they're fine."

I wonder if anything strikes you about the slice of give-and-take I've just recorded. No? Oh, surely. I mean, here were we, Stinker Pinker and Bertram Wooster, buddies who had known each other virtually from the egg, and we were talking like a couple of strangers making conversation on a train. At least, he was, and more and more I became convinced that his bosom was full of the perilous stuff that weighs upon the heart, as I remember Jeeves putting it once.

I persevered in my efforts to uncork him.

"Well, Stinker," I said, "what's new? Has Pop Bassett given you that vicarage yet?"

This caused him to open up a bit. His manner became more animated.

"No, not yet. He doesn't seem able to make up his mind. One day he says he will, the next day he says he's not so sure, he'll have to think it over."

I frowned. I disapproved of this shilly-shallying. I could see how it must be throwing a spanner into Stinker's whole foreign policy, putting him in a spot and causing him alarm and despondency. He can't marry Stiffy on a curate's stipend, so they've got to wait till Pop Bassett gives him a vicarage, which he has in his gift. And while I personally, though fond of the young gumboil, would run a mile in tight shoes to avoid marrying Stiffy, I knew him to be strongly in favor of signing her up.

"Something always happens to put him off. I think he was about ready to close the deal before he went to stay at Brinkley, but most unfortunately I bumped into a valuable vase of his and broke it. It seemed to rankle rather."

I heaved a sigh. It's always what Jeeves would call most disturbing to hear that a chap with whom you have plucked the gowans fine, as the expression is, isn't making out as well as could be wished. I was all set to follow this Pinker's career with considerable interest, but the way things were shaping it began to look as if there wasn't going to be a career to follow.

"You move in a mysterious way your wonders to perform, Stinker. I believe you would bump into something if you were crossing the Gobi desert."

"I've never been in the Gobi desert."

"Well, don't go. It isn't safe. I suppose Stiffy's sore about this . . . what's the word? . . . Not vaseline. . . . Vacillation, that's it. She chafes, I imagine, at this vacillation on Bassett's part and resents him letting 'I dare not' wait upon 'I would,' like the poor cat in the adage. Not my own, that, by the way. Jeeves'. Pretty steamed up, isn't she?"

"She is rather."

"I don't blame her. Enough to upset any girl. Pop Bassett has no right to keep gumming up the course of true love like this."

"No."

"He needs a kick in the pants."

"Yes."

"If I were Stiffy, I'd put a toad in his bed or strychnine in his soup."

"Yes. And talking of Stiffy, Bertie—"

He broke off, and I eyed him narrowly. There could be no question to my mind that I had been right about that perilous stuff. His bosom was obviously chock full of it.

"There's something the matter, Stinker."

"No, there isn't. Why do you say that?"

"Your manner is strange. You remind me of a faithful dog looking up into its proprietor's face as if it were trying to tell him something. Are you trying to tell me something?"

He swallowed once or twice, and his color deepened, which took a bit of doing, for even when his soul is in repose he always looks like a clerical beetroot. It was as though the collar he buttons at the back was choking him. In a hoarse voice he said, "Bertie."

"Hullo?"

"Bertie."

"Still here, old man, and hanging on your lips."

"Bertie, are you busy just now?"

"Not more than usual."

"You could get away for a day or two?"

"I suppose one might manage it."

"Then can you come to Totleigh?"

"To stay with you, do you mean?"

"No, to stay at Totleigh Towers."

I stared at the man, wide-eyed as the expression is. Had it not been that I knew him to be abstemiousness itself, rarely indulging in anything stronger than a light lager, and not even that during Lent, I should have leaped to the conclusion that there beside me sat a curate who had been having a couple. My eyebrows rose till they nearly disarranged my front hair.

"Stay *where?* Stinker, you're not yourself, or you wouldn't be gibbering like this. You can't have forgotten the ordeal I passed through last time I went to Totleigh Towers."

"I know. But there's something Stiffy wants you to do for her. She wouldn't tell me what it was, but she said it was most important and that you would have to be on the spot to do it."

I drew myself up. I was cold and resolute.

"You're crazy, Stinker!"

"I don't see why you say that."

"Then let me explain where your whole scheme falls to the ground. To begin with, is it likely that after what has passed between us Sir Watkyn B. would issue an invitation to one who has always been to him a pain in the neck to end all pains in the neck? If ever there was a man who was all in favor of me taking the high road while he took the low road, it is this same Bassett. His idea of a happy day is one spent with at least a hundred miles between him and Bertram."

"Madeline would invite you, if you sent her a wire asking if you could come for a day or two. She never consults Sir

Watkyn about guests. It's an understood thing that she has anyone she wants to at the house."

This I knew to be true, but I ignored the suggestion and proceeded remorselessly.

"In the second place, I know Stiffy. A charming girl whom, as I was telling Emerald Stoker, I am always prepared to clasp to my bosom—at least I would be if she wasn't engaged to you—but one who is a cross between a ticking bomb and a poltergeist. She lacks that balanced judgment which we like to see in girls. She gets ideas, and if you care to call them bizarre ideas, it will be all right with me. I need scarcely remind you that when I last visited Totleigh Towers she egged you on to pinch Constable Eustace Oates' helmet, the one thing a curate should shrink from doing if he wishes to rise to heights in the Church. She is, in short, about as loony a young shrimp as ever wore a windswept hairdo. What this commission is that she has in mind for me we cannot say, but going by the form book I see it as something totally unfit for human consumption. Didn't she even hint at its nature?"

"No. I asked, of course, but she said she would rather keep it under her hat till she saw you."

"She won't see me."

"You won't come to Totleigh?"

"Not within fifty miles of the sewage dump."

"She'll be terribly disappointed."

"You will administer spiritual solace. That's your job. Tell her these things are sent to try us."

"She'll probably cry."

"Nothing better for the nervous system. It does something, I forget what, to the glands. Ask any well-known Harley Street physician."

I suppose he saw that my iron front was not to be shaken,

for he made no further attempt to sell the idea to me. With a sigh that seemed to come up from the soles of the feet, he rose, said goodbye, knocked over the glass from which I had been refreshing myself, and withdrew.

Knowing how loath Bertram Wooster always is to let a pal down and fail him in his hour of need, you are probably thinking that this distressing scene had left me shaken, but as a matter of fact it had bucked me up like a day at the seaside.

Let's just review the situation. Ever since breakfast my guardian angel had been scaring the pants off me by practically saying in so many words that Totleigh Towers was all set to re-enter my life, and it was now clear that what he had in mind had been the imminence of this plea to me to go there, he feeling that in a weak moment I might allow myself to be persuaded against my better judgment. The peril was now past. Totleigh Towers had made its spring and missed by a mile, and I no longer had a thing to worry about. It was with a light heart that I joined a group of pleasure-seekers who were playing darts and cleaned them up with effortless skill. Three o'clock was approaching when I left the club en route for home, and it must have been getting on for half past when I hove alongside the apartment house where I have my abode.

There was a cab standing outside, laden with luggage. From its window Gussie Fink-Nottle's head was poking out, and I remember thinking once again how mistaken Emerald Stoker had been about his appearance. Seeing him steadily, if not whole, I could detect in his aspect no trace of the lamb, but he was looking so like a halibut that if he hadn't been wearing horn-rimmed spectacles, a thing halibuts seldom do, I might have supposed myself to be gazing on something AWOL from a fishmonger's slab.

I gave him a friendly yodel, and he turned the spectacles in my direction.

"Oh, hullo, Bertie," he said, "I've just been calling on you. I left a message with Jeeves. Your aunt told me to tell you she's coming to London the day after tomorrow and she wants you to give her lunch."

"Yes, she was on the phone to that effect this morning. I suppose she thought you'd forget to notify me. Come in and have some orange juice," I said, for it is to that muck that he confines himself with making whoopee.

He looked at his watch, and his eyes lost the gleam that always comes into them when orange juice is mentioned.

"I wish I could, but I can't," he sighed. "I should miss my train. I'm off to Totleigh on the four o'clock at Paddington."

"Oh, really? Well, look out for a friend of yours, who'll be on it. Emerald Stoker."

"Stoker? Stoker? Emerald Stoker?"

"Girl with freckles. American. Looks like a Pekingese of the better sort. She tells me she met you at a studio party the other day, and you talked about newts."

His face cleared.

"Of course, yes. Now I've placed her. I didn't get her name that day. Yes, we had a long talk about newts. She used to keep them herself as a child, only she called them guppies. A most delightful girl. I shall enjoy seeing her again. I don't know when I've met a girl who attracted me more."

"Except, of course, Madeline."

His face darkened. He looked like a halibut that's taken offense at a rude remark from another halibut.

"Madeline! Don't talk to me about Madeline! Madeline makes me sick!" he hissed. "Paddington!" he shouted to the charioteer, and was gone with the wind, leaving me gaping after him, all of a twitter.

CHAPTER
FOUR

AND I'LL tell you why I was all of a t. My critique of her
when chatting with Emerald Stoker will have shown how
allergic I was to this Bassett beazel. She was scarcely less of
a pain in the neck to me than I was to her father or Roderick
Spode. Nevertheless, there was a grave danger that I might
have to take her for better or for worse, as the book of rules
puts it.

The facts may be readily related. Gussie, enamored of
the Bassett, would have liked to let her in on the way he
felt, but every time he tried to do so his nerve deserted him
and he found himself babbling about newts. At a loss to
know how to swing the deal, he got the idea of asking me
to plead his cause, and when I pleaded it, the Bassett, as pronounced a fathead as ever broke biscuit, thought I was

[36]

pleading mine. She said she was so so sorry to cause me pain, but her heart belonged to Gussie. Which would have been fine, had she not gone on to say that if anything should ever happen to make her revise her conviction that he was a king among men and she was compelled to give him the heave-ho, I was the next in line, and while she could never love me with the same fervor she felt for Gussie, she would do her best to make me happy. I was, in a word, in the position of a Vice-President of the United States of America who, while feeling that he is all right so far, knows that he will be for it at a moment's notice if anything goes wrong with the man up top.

Little wonder, then, that Gussie's statement that Madeline made him sick smote me like a ton of bricks and had me indoors and bellowing for Jeeves before you could say what ho. As had so often happened before, I felt that my only course was to place myself in the hands of a higher power.

"Sir?" he said, manifesting himself.

"A ghastly thing has happened, Jeeves! Disaster looms."

"Indeed, sir? I am sorry to hear that."

There's one thing you have to give Jeeves credit for. He lets the dead past bury its d. He and the young master may have had differences about Alpine hats with pink feathers in them, but when he sees the y. m. on the receiving end of the slings and arrows of outrageous fortune, he sinks his dudgeon and comes through with the feudal spirit at its best. So now, instead of being cold and distant and aloof, as a lesser man would have been, he showed the utmost agitation and concern. That is to say, he allowed one eyebrow to rise perhaps an eighth of an inch, which is as far as he ever goes in the way of expressing emotion.

"What would appear to be the trouble, sir?"

I sank into a chair and mopped the frontal bone. Not for many a long day had I been in such a doodah.

"I've just seen Gussie Fink-Nottle."

"Yes, sir. Mr. Fink-Nottle was here a moment ago."

"I met him outside. He was in a cab. And do you know what?"

"No, sir."

"I happened to mention Miss Bassett's name, and he said—follow this closely, Jeeves—he said—I quote—'Don't talk to me about Madeline. Madeline makes me sick.' Close quotes."

"Indeed, sir?"

"Those are not the words of love."

"No, sir."

"They are the words of a man who for some reason not disclosed is fed to the front teeth with the adored object. I hadn't time to go into the matter, because a moment later he was off like a scalded cat to Paddington, but it's pretty clear there must have been a rift in the what-d' you-call-it. Begins with an l."

"Would lute be the word for which you are groping, sir?"

"Possibly. I don't know that I'd care to bet on it."

"The poet Tennyson speaks of the little rift within the lute, that by and by will make the music mute and ever widening slowly silence all."

"Then lute it is. And we know what's going to happen if this particular lute goes phut."

We exchanged significant glances. At least, I gave him a significant glance, and he looked like a stuffed frog, his habit when being discreet. He knows just how I'm situated as regards M. Bassett, but naturally we don't discuss it except by going into the sig-glance-stuffed-frog routine. I mean, you can't talk about a thing like that. I don't know if it would actually come under the head of speaking lightly of a woman's name, but it wouldn't be seemly, and the Woosters are sticklers for seemliness. So, for that matter, are the Jeeveses.

"What ought I to do, do you think?"

"Sir?"

"Don't stand there saying 'Sir?' You know as well as I do that a situation has arisen which calls for the immediate coming of all good men to the aid of the party. It is of the essence that Gussie's engagement does not spring a leak. Steps must be taken."

"It would certainly seem advisable, sir."

"But what steps? I ought, of course, to hasten to the seat of war and try to start the dove of peace going into its act—have a bash, in other words, at seeing what a calm, kindly man of the world can do to bring the young folks together, if you get what I mean."

"I apprehend you perfectly, sir. Your role, as I see it, would be that of what the French call the *raisonneur*."

"You're probably right. But mark this. Apart from the fact that the mere thought of being under the roof of Totleigh Towers again is one that freezes the gizzard, there's another snag. I was talking to Stinker Pinker just now, and he says that Stiffy Byng has something she wants me to do for her. Well, you know the sort of thing Stiffy generally wants people to do. You recall the episode of Constable Oates' helmet?"

"Very vividly, sir."

"Oates had incurred her displeasure by reporting to her Uncle Watkyn that her dog Bartholomew had spilled him off his bicycle, causing him to fall into a ditch and sustain bruises and contusions, and she persuaded Harold Pinker, a man in holy orders who buttons his collar at the back, to pinch his helmet for her. And that was comparatively mild for Stiffy. There are no limits, literally none, to what she can think of when she gives her mind to it. The imagination boggles at the thought of what she may be cooking up for me."

"Certainly you may be pardoned for feeling apprehensive, sir."

"So there you are. I'm on the horns of . . . what are those things you get on the horns of?"

"Dilemmas, sir."

"That's right. I'm on the horns of a dilemma. Shall I, I ask myself, go and see what I can accomplish in the way of running repairs on the lute, or would it be more prudent to stay put and let nature take its course, trusting to Time, the great healer, to do its stuff?"

"If I might make a suggestion, sir?"

"Press on, Jeeves."

"Would it not be possible for you to go to Totleigh Towers but to decline to carry out Miss Byng's wishes?"

I weighed this. It was, I could see, a thought.

"Issue a *nolle prosequi,* you mean? Tell her to go and boil her head?"

"Precisely, sir."

I eyed him reverently.

"Jeeves," I said, "as always, you have found the way. I'll wire Miss Bassett asking if I can come, and I'll wire Aunt Dahlia that I can't give her lunch, as I'm leaving town. And I'll tell Stiffy that whatever she has in mind, she gets no service and cooperation from me. Yes, Jeeves, you've hit it. I'll go to Totleigh, though the flesh creeps at the prospect. Pop Bassett will be there. Spode will be there. Stiffy will be there. The dog Bartholomew will be there. It makes one wonder why so much fuss has been made about those half-a-league half-a-league half-a-league-onward bimbos who rode into the Valley of Death. They weren't going to find Pop Bassett at the other end. Ah well, let us hope for the best."

"The only course to pursue, sir."

"Stiff upper lip, Jeeves, what?"

"Indubitably, sir. That, if I may say so, is the spirit."

CHAPTER
FIVE

As STINKER had predicted, Madeline Bassett placed no obstacle in the way of my visiting Totleigh Towers. In response to my invitation-cadging missive she gave me the green light, and an hour or so after her telegram had arrived Aunt Dahlia rang up from Brinkley, full of eagerness to ascertain what the hell, she having just received my wire saying that owing to absence from the metropolis I would be unable to give her the lunch for which she had been budgeting.

Her call came as no surprise. I had anticipated that there might be a certain liveliness on the Brinkley front. The old flesh and blood is a genial soul who loves her Bertram dearly, but she is a woman of imperious spirit. She dislikes having her wishes thwarted, and her voice came booming at me like a pack of hounds in full cry.

"Bertie, you foul young blot on the landscape?"

"Speaking."

"I got your telegram."

"I thought you would. Very efficient, the gramming service."

"What do you mean, you're leaving town? You never leave town except to come down here and wallow in Anatole's cooking."

Her allusion was to her peerless French chef, at the mention of whose name the mouth starts watering automatically. God's gift to the gastric juices I have sometimes called him.

"Where are you going?"

My mouth having stopped watering, I said I was going to Totleigh Towers, and she uttered an impatient snort.

"There's something wrong with this blasted wire. It sounded as if you were saying you were going to Totleigh Towers."

"I am."

"To Totleigh *Towers?*"

"I leave this afternoon."

"What in the world made them invite you?"

"They didn't. I invited myself."

"You mean you're deliberately seeking the society of Sir Watkyn Bassett? You must be more of an ass than even I have ever thought you. And I speak as a woman who has just had the old bounder in her hair for more than a week."

I saw her point, and hastened to explain.

"I admit Pop Bassett is a bit above the odds," I said, "and unless one is compelled by circumstances it is always wisest not to stir him, but a sharp crisis has been precipitated in my affairs. All is not well between Gussie Fink-Nottle and Madeline Bassett. Their engagement is tottering toward the melting pot, and you know what that engagement means to me. I'm going down there to try to heal the rift."

"What can you do?"

"My role, as I see it, will be that of what the French call the *raisonneur*."

"And what does that mean?"

"Ah, there you have me, but that's what Jeeves says I'll be."

"Are you taking Jeeves with you?"

"Of course. Do I ever stir foot without him?"

"Well, watch out, that's all I say to you; watch out. I happen to know that Bassett is making overtures to him."

"How do you mean, overtures?"

"He's trying to steal him from you."

I reeled, and might have fallen, had I not been sitting at the time.

"Incredulous!"

"If you mean incredible, you're wrong. I told you how he had fallen under Jeeves' spell when he was here. He used to follow him with his eyes as he buttled, like a cat watching a duck, as Anatole would say. And one morning I heard him making him a definite proposition. Well? What's the matter with you? Have you fainted?"

I told her that my momentary silence had been due to the fact that her words had stunned me, and she said she didn't see why, knowing Bassett, I should be so surprised.

"You can't have forgotten how he tried to steal Anatole. There isn't anything to which that man won't stoop. He has no conscience whatsoever. When you get to Totleigh, go and see someone called Plank and ask him what he thinks of Sir Watkyn ruddy Bassett. He chiseled this poor devil Plank out of a . . . Oh, hell!" said the aged relative as a voice intoned "Thur-ree minutes," and she hung up, having made my flesh creep as nimbly as if she had been my guardian angel, on whose talent in that direction I have already touched.

[44]

It was still creeping with undiminished gusto as I steered the sports model along the road to Totleigh-in-the-Wold that afternoon. I was convinced, of course, that Jeeves would never dream of severing relations with the old firm, and when urged to do so by this blighted Bassett would stop his ears like the deaf adder, which, as you probably know, made a point of refusing to hear the voice of the charmer, charm he never so wisely. But the catch is that you can be convinced about a thing and nevertheless get pretty jumpy when you muse on it, and it was in no tranquil mood that I eased the Arab steed through the gates of Totleigh Towers and fetched up at the front door.

I don't know if you happen to have come across a hymn, the chorus of which goes

> *Tum tumty tumty tumty*
> *Tum tiddly om pom isle,*
> *Where every prospect pleases*
> *And only man is vile*

or words to that effect, but the description would have fitted Totleigh Towers like the paper on the wall. Its façade, its spreading grounds, rolling parkland, smoothly shaven lawns and what not were all just like Mother makes, but what percentage was there in that, when you knew what was waiting for you inside? It's never a damn bit of use a prospect pleasing if the gang that goes with it lets it down.

This lair of old Bassett's was one of the fairly stately homes of England—not a showplace like the joints you read about with three hundred and sixty-five rooms, fifty-two staircases, and twelve courtyards, but definitely not a bungalow. He had bought it furnished some time previously from a Lord Somebody who needed cash, as so many do these days.

Not Pop Bassett, though. In the evening of his life he had more than a sufficiency. It would not be going too far, indeed, to describe him as stinking rich. For a great part of his adult life he had been a metropolitan police magistrate, and in that capacity once fined me five quid for a mere lighthearted peccadillo on Boat Race Night, when a mild reprimand would more than have met the case. It was shortly after this that a relative died and left him a vast fortune. That, at least, was the story given out. What really happened, of course, was that all through his years as a magistrate he had been trousering the fines, amassing the stuff in sackfuls. Five quid here, five quid there, it soon mounts up.

We had made goodish going on the road, and it wasn't more than about four-forty when I rang the front-door bell. Jeeves took the car to the stables, and the butler—Butterfield was his name, I remembered—led me to the drawing room.

"Mr. Wooster," he said, loosing me in.

I was not surprised to find tea in progress, for I had heard the clinking of cups. Madeline Bassett was at the controls, and she extended a drooping hand to me.

"Bertie! How nice to see you."

I can well imagine that a casual observer, if I had confided to him my qualms at the idea of being married to this girl, would have raised his eyebrows and been at a loss to understand, for she was undeniably an eyeful, being slim, svelte, and bountifully equipped with golden hair and all the fixings. But where the casual observer would have been making his bloomer was in overlooking that squashy soupiness of hers, that subtle air she had of being on the point of talking baby talk. She was the sort of girl who puts her hands over a husband's eyes, as he is crawling in to breakfast with a morning head, and says, "Guess who?"

I once stayed at the residence of a newly married pal of mine, and his bride had had carved in large letters over the fireplace in the drawing room, where it was impossible to miss it, the legend "Two Lovers Built This Nest," and I can still recall the look of dumb anguish in the other half of the sketch's eyes every time he came in and saw it. Whether Madeline Bassett, on entering the marital state, would go to such an awful extreme, one could not say, but it seemed most probable, and I resolved that when I started trying to reconcile her and Gussie, I would not scamp my work but would give it everything I had.

"You know Mr. Pinker," she said, and I perceived that Stinker was present. He was safely wedged in a chair and hadn't, as far as I could see, upset anything yet, but he gave me the impression of a man who was crouching for the spring and would begin to operate shortly. There was a gateleg table laden with muffins and cucumber sandwiches, which I foresaw would attract him like a magnet.

On seeing me, he had started visibly, dropping a plate with half a muffin on it, and his eyes had widened. I knew what he was thinking, of course. He supposed that my presence must be due to a change of heart. Rejoice with me, for I have found the sheep which was lost, he was no doubt murmuring to himself. I mourned in spirit a bit for the poor fish, knowing what a nasty knock he had coming to him when he got on to it that nothing was going to induce me to undertake whatever the foul commission might be that Stiffy had earmarked for me. On that point I was resolved to be firm, no matter what spiritual agonies he and she suffered in the process. I had long since learned that the secret of a happy and successful life was to steer clear of any project masterminded by that young scourge of the species.

The conversation that followed was what you might

call . . . I've forgotten the word, but it begins with a d. I mean, with Stinker within earshot Madeline and I couldn't get down to brass tacks, so we just chewed the fat . . . desultory, that's the word I wanted. We just chewed the fat in a desultory way. Stinker said he was there to talk over the forthcoming school treat with Sir Watkyn, and I said, "Oh, is there a school treat coming up?" And Madeline said it was taking place the day after tomorrow and owing to the illness of the vicar Mr. Pinker would be in sole charge, and Stinker winced a bit, as if he didn't like the prospect much.

Madeline asked if I had had a nice drive down, and I said, "Oh, splendid." Stinker said Stiffy would be so pleased I had come, and I smiled one of my subtle smiles. And then Butterfield came in and said Sir Watkyn could see Mr. Pinker now, and Stinker oozed off. And the moment the door had closed behind curate and butler, Madeline clasped her hands, gave me one of those squashy looks, and said:

"Oh, Bertie, you should not have come here. I had not the heart to deny your pathetic request—I knew how much you yearned to see me again, however briefly, however hopelessly—but was it *wise?* Is it not merely twisting the knife in the wound? Will it not simply cause you needless pain to be near me, knowing we can never be more than just good friends? It is useless, Bertie. You must not hope. I love Augustus."

Her words, as you may well imagine, were music to my e. She wouldn't, I felt, have come out with anything as definite as this if there had been a really serious spot of trouble between her and Gussie. Obviously that crack of his about her making him sick had been a mere passing what-d'-you-call-it, the result of some momentary attack of the pip caused possibly by her saying he smoked too much or something of the sort. Anyway, whatever it was that had rifted the lute was now plainly forgotten and forgiven, and I was saying to myself that, the way things looked, I ought to be able to duck out of here immediately after breakfast tomorrow, when I noticed that a look of pain had spread over her map and that the eyes were dewy.

"It makes me so sad to think of your hopeless love, Bertie," she said, adding something which I didn't quite catch about moths and stars. "Life is so tragic, so cruel. But what can I do?"

"Not a thing," I said heartily. "Just carry on regardless."

"But it breaks my heart."

And with these words she burst into what are sometimes called uncontrollable sobs. She sank into her chair, covering her face with her hands, and it seemed to me that the civil thing to do was to pat her head. This project I now carried out, and I can see, looking back, that it was a mistake. I remember Monty Bodkin of the Drones, who once patted a weeping female on the head, unaware that his betrothed was standing in his immediate rear, drinking the whole thing in, telling me that the catch in this head-patting routine is that, unless you exercise the greatest care, you forget to take your hand off. You just stand there resting it on the subject's bean, and this is apt to cause spectators to purse their lips.

Monty fell into this error and so did I. And the lip-pursing was attended to by Spode, who chanced to enter at this moment. Seeing the popsy bathed in tears, he quivered from stem to stern.

"Madeline!" he yipped. "What's the matter?"

"It is nothing, Roderick, nothing," she replied chokingly.

She buzzed off, no doubt to bathe her eyes, and Spode pivoted round and gave me a penetrating look. He had grown a bit, I noticed, since I had last seen him, being now about nine foot seven. In speaking of him to Emerald Stoker I had, if you remember, compared him to a gorilla, and what I had had in mind had been the ordinary run-of-the-mill gorilla, not the large economy size. What he was looking like now was King Kong. His fists were clenched, his eyes glittered, and the dullest observer could have divined that it was in no sunny spirit that he was regarding Bertram.

CHAPTER
SIX

To EASE the strain, I asked him if he would have a cucumber sandwich, but with an impassioned gesture he indicated that he was not in the market for cucumber sandwiches, though I could have told him, for I had found them excellent, that he was passing up a good thing.

"A muffin?"

No, not a muffin, either. He seemed to be on a diet.

"Wooster," he said, his jaw muscles moving freely, "I can't make up my mind whether to break your neck or not."

"Not" would have been the way my vote would have been cast, but he didn't give me time to say so.

"I was amazed when I heard from Madeline that you had had the effrontery to invite yourself here. Your motive, of course, was clear. You have come to try to undermine her faith in the man she loves and sow doubts in her mind. Like a creeping snake," he added, and I was interested to learn that this was what snakes did. "You had not the elementary decency, when she had made her choice, to accept her decision and efface yourself. You hoped to win her away from Fink-Nottle."

Feeling that it was about time I said something, I got as far as "I," but he shushed me with another of those impassioned gestures. I couldn't remember when I'd met anyone so resolved on hogging the conversation.

"No doubt you will say that your love was so overpowering that you could not resist the urge to tell her of it and plead with her. Utter nonsense. Despicable weakness. Let me tell you, Wooster, that I have loved that girl for years and years, but never by word or look have I so much as hinted it to her. It was a great shock to me when she became engaged to this man Fink-Nottle, but I accepted the situation because I thought that that was where her happiness lay. Though stunned, I kept—"

"A stiff upper lip?"

"—my feelings to myself. I sat—"

"Like Patience on a monument."

"—tight, and said nothing that would give her a suspicion of how I felt. All that mattered was that she should be happy. If you ask me if I approve of Fink-Nottle as a husband for her, I admit frankly that I do not. To me he seems to possess all the qualities that go to make the perfect pill, and I may add that my opinon is shared by her father. But he is the man she has chosen and I abide by her choice. I do not crawl behind Fink-Nottle's back and try to prejudice her against him."

"Very creditable."

[52]

"What did you say?"

I said I had said it did him credit. Very white of him, I said I thought it.

"Oh? Well, I suggest to you, Wooster, that you follow my example. And let me tell you that I shall be watching you closely, and I shall expect to see less of this head-stroking you were doing when I came in. If I don't, I'll—"

Just what he proposed to do he did not reveal, though I was able to hazard a guess, for at this moment Madeline returned. Her eyes were pinkish and her general aspect down among the wines and spirits.

"I will show you your room, Bertie," she said in a pale, saintlike voice, and Spode gave me a warning look.

"Be careful, Wooster, be very careful," he said as we went out.

Madeline seemed surprised.

"Why did Roderick tell you to be careful?"

"Ah, that we shall never know. Afraid I might slip on the parquet floor, do you think?"

"He sounded as if he was angry with you. Had you been quarreling?"

"Good heavens, no. Our talk was conducted throughout in an atmosphere of the utmost cordiality."

"I thought he might be annoyed at your coming here."

"On the contrary. Nothing could have exceeded the warmth of his 'Welcome to Totleigh Towers.' "

"I'm so glad. It would pain me so much if you and he were . . . Oh, there's Daddy."

We had reached the upstairs corridor, and Sir Watkyn Bassett was emerging from his room, humming a light air. It died on his lips as he saw me, and he stood staring at me aghast. He reminded me of one of those fellows who spend the night in haunted houses and are found next morning dead to the last drop with a look of awful horror on their faces.

"Oh, Daddy," said Madeline. "I forgot to tell you. I asked Bertie to come here for a few days."

Pop Bassett swallowed painfully.

"When you say a few days—?"

"At least a week, I hope."

"Good God!"

"If not longer."

"Great heavens!"

"There is tea in the drawing room, Daddy."

"I need something stronger than tea," said Pop Bassett in a low, husky voice, and he tottered off, a broken man. The sight of his head disappearing as he made for the lower regions where the snootful awaited him brought to my mind a poem I used to read as a child. I've forgotten most of it, but it was about a storm at sea and the punch line ran " 'We are lost,' the captain shouted, as he staggered down the stairs."

"Daddy seems upset about something," said Madeline.

"He did convey that impression," I said, speaking austerely, for the old blister's attitude had offended me. I could make allowances for him, because naturally a man of regular habits doesn't like suddenly finding Woosters in his midst, but I did feel that he might have made more of an effort to bear up. Think of the Red Indians, Bassett, I would have said to him, had we been on better terms, pointing out that they were never in livelier spirits than when being cooked on both sides at the stake.

This painful encounter, following so quickly on my conversation, if you could call it a conversation, with Spode, might have been expected to depress me, but this was far from being the case. I was so uplifted by the official news that all was well between M. Bassett and G. Fink-Nottle that I gave it little thought. It's never, of course, the ideal setup to come to stay at a house where your host shudders to the depths of his being at the mere sight of you and is compelled to rush to where the bottles are and get a restorative, but the Woosters can take the rough with the s., and the bonging of the gong for dinner some little time later found me in excellent fettle. It was to all intents and purposes with a song on my lips that I straightened my tie and made my way to the trough.

Dinner is usually the meal at which you catch Bertram at his best, and certainly it's the meal I always most enjoy. Many of my happiest hours have been passed in the society of the soup, the fish, the pheasant or whatever it may be, the soufflé, the fruits in their season, and the spot of port to follow. They bring out the best in me. "Wooster," those who know me have sometimes said, "may be a pretty total loss during the daytime hours, but plunge the world in darkness, switch on the soft lights, uncork the champagne, and shove a dinner into him, and you'd be surprised."

But if I am to sparkle and charm all and sundry, I make one proviso—viz., that the company be congenial. And anything less congenial than the co. on this occasion I have seldom encountered. Sir Watkyn Bassett, who was plainly still much shaken at finding me on the premises, was very far from being the jolly old squire who makes the party go from the start. Beyond shooting glances at me over his glasses, blinking as if he couldn't bring himself to believe I was real, and looking away with a quick shudder, he contributed little or nothing to what I have heard Jeeves call the feast of reason and the flow of soul. Add Spode, strong and silent, Madeline Bassett, mournful and drooping, Gussie, also apparently mournful, and Stiffy, who seemed to be in a kind of daydream, and you had something resembling a wake of the less rollicking type.

Somber, that's the word I was trying to think of. The atmosphere was somber. The whole binge might have been a scene from one of those Russian plays my Aunt Agatha sometimes makes me take her son Thos to at the Old Vic in order to improve his mind, which, as is widely known, can do with all the improvement that's coming to it.

It was toward the middle of the meal that, feeling that it was about time somebody said something, I drew Pop Bassett's attention to the table's centerpiece. In any normal house it would have been a bowl of flowers or something on that order, but this being Totleigh Towers it was a small black figure carved of some material I couldn't put a name to. It was so gosh-awful in every respect that I presumed it must be something he had collected recently. My Uncle Tom is always coming back from sales with similar eyesores.

"That's new, isn't it?" I said, and he started violently. I suppose he'd just managed to persuade himself that I was merely a mirage and had been brought up with a round turn on discovering that I was there in the flesh.

"That thing in the middle of the table that looks like the end man in a minstrel show. It's something you got since . . . er . . . since I was here last, isn't it?"

Tactless of me, I suppose, to remind him of that previous visit of mine, and I oughtn't to have brought it up, but these things slip out.

"Yes," he said, having paused for a moment to shudder. "It is the latest addition to my collection."

"Daddy bought it from a man named Plank who lives not far from here at Hockley-cum-Meston," said Madeline.

[56]

"Attractive little bijou," I said. It hurt me to look at it, but I felt that nothing was to be lost by giving him the old oil. "Just the sort of thing Uncle Tom would like to have. By Jove," I said, remembering, "Aunt Dahlia was speaking to me about it on the phone yesterday, and she told me Uncle Tom would give his eyeteeth to have it in his collection. I'm not surprised. It looks valuable."

"It's worth a thousand pounds," said Stiffy, coming out of her coma and speaking for the first time.

"As much as that? Golly!" Amazing, I was thinking, that magistrates could get to be able to afford expenditure on that scale just by persevering through the years fining people and sticking to the money. "What is it? Soapstone?"

I had said the wrong thing.

"Amber," Pop Bassett snapped, giving me the sort of look he had given me in heaping measure on the occasion when I had stood in the dock before him at Bosher Street Police Court. "Black amber."

"Of course, yes. That's what Aunt Dahlia said, I recall. She spoke very highly of it, let me tell you, extremely highly."

"Indeed?"

"Oh, absolutely."

I had been hoping that this splash of dialogue would have broken the ice, so to speak, and started us off kidding back and forth like the guys and dolls in one of those old-world salons you read about. But no. Silence fell again, and eventually, at long last, the meal came to an end, and two minutes later I was on my way to my room, where I proposed to pass the rest of the evening with an Erle Stanley Gardner I'd brought with me. No sense, as I saw it, in going and mixing with the mob in the drawing room and having Spode glare at me and Pop Bassett sniff at me and Madeline Bassett as likely as not sing old English folk songs at me till bedtime. I was aware that in executing this quiet sneak I was being guilty of a social gaffe which would have drawn raised eyebrows from the author of a book of etiquette, but the great lesson we learn from life is to know when and when not to be in the center of things.

CHAPTER
SEVEN

I HAVEN'T mentioned it till now, having been all tied up
with other matters, but during dinner, as you may well
imagine, something had been puzzling me not a little—the
mystery, to wit, of what on earth had become of Emerald
Stoker.

At that lunch of ours she had told me in no uncertain
terms that she was off to Totleigh on the four o'clock train
that afternoon, and, however leisurely its progress, it must
have got there by this time, because Gussie had traveled on
it and he had fetched up at the joint all right. But I could
detect no sign of her on the premises. It seemed to me, sift-
ing the evidence, that only one conclusion could be arrived
at—that she had been pulling the Wooster leg.

But why? With what motive? That was what I was asking

myself as I sneaked up the stairs to where Erle Stanley Gardner awaited me. If you had cared to describe me as perplexed and bewildered, you would have been perfectly correct.

Jeeves was in my room when I got there, going about his gentleman's gentlemanly duties, and I put my problem up to him.

"Did you ever see a film called *The Vanishing Lady,* Jeeves?"

"No, sir. I rarely attend cinematographic performances."

"Well, it was about a lady who vanished, if you follow what I mean, and the reason I bring it up is that a female friend of mine has apparently disappeared into thin air, leaving not a wrack behind, as I once heard you put it."

"Highly mysterious, sir."

"You said it. I seek in vain for a solution. When I gave her lunch yesterday, she told me she was off on the four o'clock train to go and stay at Totleigh Towers, and the point I want to drive home is that she hasn't arrived. You remember the day I lunched at the Ritz?"

"Yes, sir. You were wearing an Alpine hat."

"There is no need to dwell on the Alpine hat, Jeeves."

"No, sir."

"If you really want to know, several fellows at the Drones asked me where I had got it."

"No doubt with a view to avoiding your hatter, sir."

I saw that nothing was to be gained by bandying words. I turned the conversation to a pleasanter and less controversial subject.

"Well, Jeeves, you'll be glad to hear that everything's all right."

"Sir?"

"About that lute we were speaking of. No rift. Sound as a bell. I have it straight from the horse's mouth that Miss

Bassett and Gussie are sweethearts still. The relief is stupendous."

I hadn't expected him to clap his hands and leap about, because of course he never does, but I wasn't prepared for the way he took this bit of hot news. He failed altogether to string along with my jocund mood.

"I fear, sir, that you are too sanguine. Miss Bassett's attitude may well be such as you have described, but on Mr. Fink-Nottle's side, I am sorry to say, there exists no little dissatisfaction and resentment."

The smile which had been splitting my face faded. It's never easy to translate what Jeeves says into basic English, but I had been able to grab this one off the bat, and what I believe the French call a *frisson* went through me like a dose of salts.

"You mean she's a sweetheart still, but he isn't?"

"Precisely, sir. I encountered Mr. Fink-Nottle in the stable yard as I was putting away the car, and he confided his troubles to me. His story occasioned me grave uneasiness."

Another *frisson* passed through my frame. I had the unpleasant feeling you get sometimes that centipedes in large numbers are sauntering up and down your spinal column. I feared the worst.

"But what's happened?" I faltered, if faltered's the word.

"I regret to inform you, sir, that Miss Bassett has insisted on Mr. Fink-Nottle adopting a vegetarian diet. His mood is understandably disgruntled and rebellious."

I tottered. In my darkest hour I had never anticipated anything as bad as this. You wouldn't think it to look at him, because he's small and shrimplike and never puts on weight, but Gussie loves food. Watching him tucking into his rations at the Drones, a tapeworm would raise its hat respectfully, knowing that it was in the presence of a master.

Cut him off, therefore, from the roasts and boileds and particularly from cold steak and kidney pie, a dish of which he is inordinately fond, and you turned him into something fit for treasons, stratagems, and spoils, as the fellow said— the sort of chap who would break an engagement as soon as look at you. At the moment of my entry I had been about to light a cigarette, and now the lighter fell from my nerveless hand.

"She's made him become a *vegetarian?*"

"So Mr. Fink-Nottle informed me, sir."

"No chops?"

"No, sir."

"No steaks?"

"No, sir."

"Just spinach and similar garbage?"

"So I gather, sir."

"But why?"

"I understand that Miss Bassett has recently been reading the life of the poet Shelley, sir, and has become converted to his view that the consumption of flesh foods is unspiritual. The poet Shelley held strong opinions on this subject."

I picked up the lighter in a sort of trance. I was aware that Madeline B. was as potty as they come in the matter of stars and rabbits and what happened when fairies blew their wee noses, but I had never dreamed that her goofiness would carry her to such lengths as this. But as the picture rose before my eyes of Gussie at the dinner table picking with clouded brow at what had unquestionably looked like spinach, I knew that his story must be true. No wonder Gussie in agony of spirit had said that Madeline made him sick. Just so might a python at a zoo have spoken of its keeper, had the latter suddenly started feeding it cheese straws in lieu of the daily rabbit.

"But this is frightful, Jeeves!"

"Certainly somewhat disturbing, sir."

"If Gussie is seething with revolt, anything may happen."

"Yes, sir."

"Is there nothing we can do?"

"It might be possible for you to reason with Miss Bassett, sir. You would have a talking point. Medical research has established that the ideal diet is one in which animal and vegetable foods are balanced. A strict vegetarian diet is not recommended by the majority of doctors, as it lacks sufficient protein and in particular does not contain the protein which is built up of the amino acids required by the body. Competent observers have traced some cases of mental disorder to this shortage."

"You'd tell her that?"

"It might prove helpful, sir."

"I doubt it," I said, blowing a despondent smoke ring. "I don't think it would sway her."

"Nor on consideration do I, sir. The poet Shelley regarded the matter from the humanitarian standpoint rather than that of bodily health. He held that we should show reverence for other life-forms, and it is his views that Miss Bassett has absorbed."

A hollow groan escaped me.

"Curse the poet Shelley! I hope he trips over a loose shoelace and breaks his ruddy neck."

"Too late, sir. He is no longer with us."

"Blast all vegetables!"

"Yes, sir. Your concern is understandable. I may mention that the cook expressed herself in a somewhat similar vein when I informed her of Mr. Fink-Nottle's predicament. Her heart melted in sympathy with his distress."

I was in no mood to hear about cooks' hearts, soluble

or otherwise, and I was about to say so when he proceeded.

"She instructed me to apprise Mr. Fink-Nottle that if he were agreeable to visiting the kitchen at some late hour when the household had retired for the night, she would be happy to supply him with cold steak and kidney pie."

It was as if the sun had come smiling through the clouds or the long shot on which I had placed my wager had nosed its way past the opposition in the last ten yards and won by a short head. For the peril that had threatened to split the Bassett–Fink-Nottle axis had been averted. I knew Gussie from soup to nuts. Cut him off from the proteins and the amino acids, and you soured his normally amiable nature, turning him into a sullen hater of his species who asked nothing better than to bite his n. and dearest and bite them good. But give him this steak and kidney pie outlet, thus allowing him to fulfill what they call his legitimate aspirations, and chagrin would vanish and he would become his old lovable self once more. The dark scowl would be replaced by the tender simper, the acid crack by the honeyed word, and all would be hotsy-totsy once more with his love life. My bosom swelled with gratitude to the cook whose quick thinking had solved the problem and brought home the bacon.

"Who is she, Jeeves?"

"Sir?"

"This life-saving cook. I shall want to give her a special mention in my evening prayers."

"She is a woman of the name of Stoker, sir."

"*Stoker?* Did you say Stoker?"

"Yes, sir."

"Odd!"

"Sir?"

"Nothing. Just a rather strange coincidence. Have you told Gussie?"

"Yes, sir. I found him most cooperative. He plans to present himself in the kitchen shortly after midnight. Cold steak and kidney pie is, of course, merely a palliative—"

"On the contrary. It's Gussie's favorite dish. I've known him to order it even on curry day at the Drones. He loves the stuff."

"Indeed, sir? That is very gratifying."

"Gratifying is the word. What a lesson this teaches us, Jeeves—never to despair, never to throw in the towel and turn our face to the wall, for there is always hope."

"Yes, sir. Would you be requiring anything further?"

"Not a thing, thanks. My cup runneth over."

"Then I will be saying good night, sir."

"Good night, Jeeves."

After he had gone, I put in about half an hour on my Erle Stanley Gardner, but I found rather a difficulty in following the thread and keeping my attention on the clues. My thoughts kept straying to this epoch-making cook. Strange, I felt, that her name should be Stoker. Some relation, perhaps.

I could picture the woman so exactly. Stout, red-faced, spectacled, a little irritable, perhaps, if interrupted when baking a cake or thinking out a sauce, but soft as butter at heart. No doubt something in Gussie's wan aspect had touched her ("That boy needs feeding up, poor little fellow"), or possibly she was fond of goldfish and had been drawn to him because he reminded her of them. Or she may have been a Girl Guide. At any rate, whatever the driving motive behind her day's good deed, she had deserved well of Bertram, and I told myself that a thumping tip should reward her on my departure. Purses of gold should be scattered, and with a lavish hand.

I was musing thus and feeling more benevolent every minute, when who should blow in but Gussie in person, and

I had been right in picturing his aspect as wan. He wore the unmistakable look of a man who has been downing spinach for weeks.

I took it that he had come to ask me what I was doing at Totleigh Towers, a point on which he might naturally be supposed to be curious, but that didn't seem to interest him. He plunged without delay into as forceful a denunciation of the vegetable world as I've ever heard, oddly enough being more bitter about Brussels sprouts and broccoli than about spinach, which I would have expected him to feature. It was some considerable time before I could get a word in, but when I did my voice dripped with sympathy.

"Yes, Jeeves was telling me about that," I said, "and my heart bled for you."

"And so it jolly well ought to have done—in buckets—if you've a spark of humanity in you," he retorted warmly. "Words cannot describe the agonies I've suffered, particularly when staying at Brinkley Court."

I nodded. I knew just what an ordeal it must have been. With Aunt Dahlia's peerless chef wielding the skillet, the last place where you want to be on a vegetarian diet is Brinkley. Many a time when enjoying the old relative's hospitality I've regretted that I had only one stomach to give to the evening's bill of fare.

"Night after night I had to refuse Anatole's unbeatable eatables, and when I tell you that two nights in succession he gave us those Mignonettes de Poulet Petit Duc of his and on another occasion his Timbales de Ris de Veau Toulousaine, you will appreciate what I went through."

It being my constant policy to strew a little happiness as I go by, I hastened to point out the silver lining in the c's.

"Your sufferings must have been terrible," I agreed. "But courage, Gussie. Think of the cold steak and kidney pie."

I had struck the right note. His drawn face softened.

"Jeeves told you about that?"

"He said the cook had it all ready and waiting for you, and I remember thinking at the time that she must be a pearl among women."

"That is not putting it at all too strongly. She's an angel in human shape. I spotted her solid merits the moment I saw her."

"You've seen her?"

"Of course I've seen her. You can't have forgotten that talk we had when I was in the cab, about to start off for Paddington. Though why you should have got the idea that she looks like a Pekingese is more than I can imagine."

"Eh? Who?"

"Emerald Stoker. She doesn't look in the least like a Pekingese."

"What's Emerald Stoker got to do with it?"

He seemed surprised.

"Didn't she tell you?"

"Tell me what?"

"That she was on her way here to take office as the Totleigh Towers cook."

I goggled. I thought for a moment that the privations through which he was passing must have unhinged this newt fancier's brain.

"Did you say *cook?*"

"I'm surprised she didn't tell you. I suppose she felt that you weren't to be trusted to keep her secret. She would, of course, have spotted you as a babbler from the outset. Yes, she's the cook all right."

"But *why* is she the cook?" I said, getting down to the *res* in that direct way of mine.

"She explained that fully to me on the train. It appears that she's dependent on a monthly allowance from her father in New York, and normally she gets by reasonably comfortably on this. But early this month she was unfortunate in her investments on the turf. Sunny Jim in the three o'clock at Kempton Park."

I recalled the horse to which he referred. Only prudent second thoughts had kept me from having a bit on it myself.

"The animal ran sixth in a field of seven and she lost her little all. She was then faced with the alternative of applying to her father for funds, which would have necessitated a full confession of her rash act, or of seeking some gainful occupation which would tide her over till, as she put it, the United States Marines arrived."

"She could have touched me or her sister Pauline."

"My good ass, a girl like that doesn't borrow money. Much too proud. She decided to become a cook. She tells me she didn't hesitate more than about thirty seconds before making her choice."

I wasn't surprised. To have come clean to the paternal parent would have been to invite hell of the worst description. Old Stoker was not the type of father who laughs indulgently when informed by a daughter that she has lost her chemise and foundation garments at the races. I don't suppose he has ever laughed indulgently in his life. I've never seen him even smile. Apprised of his child's goings-on, he would unquestionably have blown his top and reduced her to the level of a fifth-rate power. I have been present on occasions when the old gawd-help-us was going good, and I can testify that his boiling point is low. Quite rightly had she decided that silence was best.

It was quite a load off my mind to be able to file away the Emerald Stoker mystery in my casebook as solved, for I dislike being baffled and the thing had been weighing on me, but there were one or two small points to be cleared up.

"How did she happen to come to Totleigh?"

"I must have been responsible for that. During our talk at that studio party, I remember mentioning that Sir Watkyn was in the market for a cook, and I suppose I must have given her his address, for she applied for the post and got it. These American girls have such enterprise."

"Is she enjoying her job?"

"Thoroughly, according to Jeeves. She's teaching the butler rummy."

"I hope she skins him to the bone."

"No doubt she will when he is sufficiently advanced to play for money. And she tells me she loves to cook. What's her cooking like?"

I could answer that. She had once or twice given me dinner at her flat, and the browsing had been impeccable.

"It melts in the mouth."

"It hasn't melted in mine," said Gussie bitterly. "Ah well," he added, a softer light coming into his eyes, "there's always that steak and kidney pie."

And on this happier note he took his departure.

CHAPTER
EIGHT

IT WAS pretty late when I finished the perusal of my Erle Stanley Gardner and later when I woke from the light doze into which I had fallen on closing the volume. Totleigh Towers had long since called it a day, and all was still throughout the house except for a curious rumbling noise proceeding from my interior. After bending an ear to this for a while, I was able to see what was causing it. I had fed sparsely at the dinner table, with the result that I had become as hungry as dammit.

I don't know if you have had the same experience, but a thing I've always found about myself is that it takes very little to put me off my feed. Let the atmosphere at lunch or dinner be what you might call difficult, and my appetite tends to dwindle. I've often had this happen when breaking bread with my Aunt Agatha, and it had happened again at tonight's meal. What with the strain of constantly catching Pop Bassett's eye and looking hastily away and catching Spode's and looking hastily away and catching Pop's again, I had done far less than justice to Emerald Stoker's no doubt admirable offerings. You read stories sometimes where someone merely toys with his food or even pushes away his plate untasted, and that substantially was what I had done. So now this strange hollow feeling, as if some hidden hand had scooped out my insides with a tablespoon.

This imperative demand for sustenance had probably been coming on during my Erle Stanley Gardnering, but I had been so intent on trying to keep tab on the murder gun and the substitute gun and the gun which Perry Mason had buried in the shrubbery that I hadn't noticed it. Only now had the pangs of hunger really started to throw their weight about, and more and more clearly as they did so there rose before my eyes the vision of that steak and kidney pie which was lurking in the kitchen, and it was as though I could hear a soft voice calling to me, "Come and get it."

It's odd how often you find that out of evil cometh good, as the expression is. Here was a case in point. I had always thought of my previous visit to Totleigh Towers as a total loss. I saw now that I had been wrong. It had been an ordeal testing the nervous system to the utmost, but there was one thing about it to be placed on the credit side of the ledger. I allude to the fact that it had taught me the way to the kitchen. The route lay down the stairs, through the hall, into the dining room, and through the door at the end of the last named. Beyond the door I presumed that there was some sort of passage or corridor and then you were in the steak and kidney pie zone. A simple journey, not to be compared for complexity with some I had taken at night in my time.

With the Woosters to think is to act, and scarcely more than two minutes later I was on my way.

It was dark on the stairs and just as dark, if not darker, in the hall. But I was making quite satisfactory progress and was about halfway through the latter when an unforeseen hitch occurred. I bumped into a human body, the last thing I had expected to encounter en route, and for an instant . . . well, I won't say that everything went black, because everything was black already, but I was considerably perturbed. My heart did one of those spectacular leaps Nijinsky used to do in the Russian Ballet, and I was conscious of a fervent wish that I could have been elsewhere.

Elsewhere, however, being just where I wasn't, I had no option but to grapple with this midnight marauder, and when I did so I was glad to find that he was apparently one who had stunted his growth by smoking as a boy. There was a shrimplike quality about him which I found most encouraging. It seemed to me that it would be an easy task to throttle him into submission, and I was getting down to it with a hearty goodwill when my hand touched what were plainly spectacles and at the same moment a stifled "Hey, look out for my glasses!" told me my diagnosis had been all wrong. This was no thief in the night but an old crony with whom in boyhood days I had often shared my last bar of milk chocolate.

"Oh, hullo, Gussie," I said. "Is that you? I thought you were a burglar."

There was a touch of asperity in his voice as he replied: "Well, I wasn't."

"No, I see that now. Pardonable mistake, though, you must admit."

[72]

"You nearly gave me heart failure."

"I, too, was somewhat taken aback. No one more surprised than the undersigned when you suddenly popped up. I thought I had a clear track."

"Where to?"

"Need you ask? The steak and kidney pie. If you've left any."

"Yes, there's quite a bit left."

"Was it good?"

"Delicious."

"Then I think I'll be getting along. Good night, Gussie. Sorry you were troubled."

Continuing on my way, I think I must have lost my bearings a little. Shaken, no doubt, by the recent encounter. These get-togethers take their toll. At any rate, to cut a long story s., what happened was that as I felt my way along the wall I collided with what turned out to be a grandfather clock, for the existence of which I had not budgeted, and it toppled over with a sound like the delivery of several tons of coal through the roof of a conservatory. Glass crashed, pulleys and things parted from their moorings, and as I stood trying to separate my heart from the front teeth in which it had become entangled, the lights flashed on and I beheld Sir Watkyn Bassett.

It was a moment fraught with embarrassment. It's bad enough to be caught by your host prowling about his house after hours even when said host is a warm admirer and close personal friend, and I have, I think, made it clear that Pop Bassett was not one of my fans. He could barely stand the sight of me by daylight, and I suppose I looked even worse to him at one o'clock in the morning.

My feeling of having been slapped between the eyes with a custard pie was deepened by the spectacle of his dressing gown. He was a small man . . . you got the impression, seeing him, that when they were making magistrates there wasn't enough material left over when they came to him . . . and for some reason not easy to explain it nearly always happens that the smaller the ex-magistrate, the louder the dressing gown. His was a bright-purple number with yellow frogs, and I am not deceiving my public when I say that it smote me like a blow, rendering me speechless.

Not that I'd have felt chatty even if he had been up-holstered in something quiet in dark blue. I don't believe you can ever be completely at your ease in the company of some-one before whom you've stood in the dock saying "Yes, your worship" and "No, your worship" and being told by him that you're extremely lucky to get off with a fine and not fourteen days without the option. This is particularly so if you have just smashed a grandfather clock whose wel-fare is no doubt very near his heart. At any rate, be that as it may, he was the one to open the conversation, not me.

"Good God!" he said, speaking with every evidence of horror. "You!"

A thing I never know, and probably never will, is what to say when somebody says "You!" to me. A mild "Oh, hullo" was the best I could do on this occasion, and I felt at the time it wasn't good. Better, of course, than "What ho, there, Bassett!" but nevertheless not good.

"Might I ask what you are doing here at this hour, Mr. Wooster?"

Well, I might have laughed a jolly laugh and replied, "Upsetting grandfather clocks," keeping it light, as it were, if you know what I mean, but something told me it wouldn't go so frightfully well. I had what amounted to an inspira-tion.

"I came down to get a book. I'd finished my Erle Stanley

Gardner and I couldn't seem to drop off to sleep, so I came to see if I couldn't pick up something from your shelves. And in the dark I bumped into the clock."

"Indeed?" he said, putting a wealth of sniffiness into the word. A thing about this undersized little son of a bachelor I ought to have mentioned earlier is that during his career on the bench he was one of those unpleasant sarcastic magistrates who get themselves so disliked by the criminal classes. You know the type. Their remarks are generally printed in the evening papers with the word "laughter" after them in brackets, and they count the day lost when they don't make some unfortunate pickpocket or some wretched drunk and disorderly feel like a piece of cheese. I know that on the occasion when we stood face to face in Bosher Street Police Court he convulsed the audience with three solid yaks at my expense in the first two minutes, bathing me in confusion. "Indeed?" he said. "Might I inquire why you were conducting your literary researches in the dark? It would surely have been well within the scope of even your limited abilities to press a light switch."

He had me there, of course. The best I could say was that I hadn't thought of it, and he sniffed a nasty sniff, as much as to suggest that I was just the sort of dead-from-the-neck-up dumb brick who wouldn't have thought of it. He then turned to the subject of the clock, one which I would willingly have left unventilated. He said he had always valued it highly, it being more or less the apple of his eye.

"My father bought it many years ago. He took it everywhere with him."

Here again I might have lightened things by asking him if his parent wouldn't have found it simpler to have worn a wristwatch, but I felt once more that he was not in the mood.

"My father was in the diplomatic service and was constantly transferred from one post to another. He was never parted from the clock. It accompanied him in perfect safety from Rome to Vienna, from Vienna to Paris, from Paris to Washington, from Washington to Lisbon. One would have said it was indestructible. But it had still to pass the supreme test of encountering Mr. Wooster, and that was too much for it. It did not occur to Mr. Wooster . . . one cannot think of everything . . . that light may be obtained by pressing a light switch, so he—"

Here he broke off, not so much because he had finished what he had to say as because at this point in the conversation I sprang on to the top of a large chest which stood some six or seven feet distant from the spot where we were chewing the fat. I may have touched the ground once while in transit, but not more than once and that once not willingly. A cat on hot bricks could not have moved with greater nippiness.

My motives in doing so were founded on a solid basis. Toward the later stages of his observations on the clock I had gradually become aware of a curious sound, as if someone in the vicinity was gargling mouthwash, and looking about me I found myself gazing into the eyes of the dog Bartholomew, which were fixed on me with the sinister intentness which is characteristic of this breed of animal. Aberdeen terriers, possibly owing to their heavy eyebrows, always seem to look at you as if they were in the pulpit of the church of some particularly strict Scottish sect and you were a parishioner of dubious reputation sitting in the front row of the stalls.

Not that I noticed his eyes very much, my attention being riveted on his teeth. He had an excellent set and was baring them, and all I had ever heard of his tendency to bite first and ask questions afterwards passed through my mind in a flash. Hence the leap for life. The Woosters are courageous, but they do not take chances.

Pop Bassett was plainly nonplussed, and it was only when his gaze, too, fell upon Bartholomew that he abandoned what must have been his original theory—that Bertram had cracked under the strain and would do well to lose no time in seeing a good mental specialist. He eyed Bartholomew coldly and addressed him as if he had been up before him in his police court.

"Go away, sir! Lie down, sir! Go away!" he said, rasping, if that's the word.

Well, I could have told him that you can't talk to an Aberdeen terrier in that tone of voice for, except perhaps for Doberman pinschers, there is no breed of dog quicker to take offense.

"Really, the way my niece allows this infernal animal to roam at large about the——"

"House" I suppose he was about to say, but the word remained unspoken. It was a moment for rapid action, not for speech. The gargling noise had increased in volume, and Bartholomew was flexing his muscles and getting under way. He moved, he stirred, he seemed to feel the rush of life along his keel, as the fellow said, and Pop Bassett, with a lissomeness of which I would not have suspected him, took to himself the wings of the dove and floated down beside me on the chest. Whether he clipped a second or two off my time I cannot say, but I rather think he did.

"This is intolerable!" he said as I moved courteously to make room for him, and I could see the thing from his point of view. All he asked from life, now that he had made his pile, was to be as far away as possible from Bertram Wooster, and here he was cheek by jowl, as you might say, on a rather uncomfortable chest with him. A certain peevishness was inevitable.

"Not too good," I agreed. "Unquestionably open to criticism, the animal's behavior."

"He must be off his head. He knows me perfectly well. He sees me every day."

"Ah," I said, putting my finger on the weak spot in his argument, "but I don't suppose he's ever seen you in that dressing gown."

I had been too outspoken. He let me see at once that he had taken umbrage.

"What's wrong with my dressing gown?" he demanded hotly.

"A bit on the bright side, don't you think?"

"No, I do not."

"Well, that's how it would strike a high-strung dog."

I paused here to chuckle softly, and he asked what the devil I was giggling about. I put him abreast.

"I was merely thinking that I wish we *could* strike the high-strung dog. The trouble on these occasions is that one is always weaponless. It was the same some years ago when an angry swan chased self and friend on to the roof of a sort of boathouse building at my Aunt Agatha's place in Hertfordshire. Nothing would have pleased us better than to bung a brick at the bird, or slosh him with a boathook, but we had no brick and were short of boathooks. We had to wait till Jeeves came along, which he eventually did in answer to our cries. It would have thrilled you to have seen Jeeves on that occasion. He advanced dauntlessly and—"

"Mr. Wooster!"

"Speaking."

"Kindly spare me your reminiscences."

"I was merely saying—"

"Well, don't."

Silence fell. On my part, a wounded silence, for all I'd tried to do was take his mind off things with entertaining chitchat. I moved an inch or two away from him in a marked manner. The Woosters do not force their conversation on the unwilling.

All this time Bartholomew had been trying to join us, making a series of energetic springs. Fortunately Providence in its infinite wisdom had given Scotties short legs, and though full of the will to win he could accomplish nothing constructive. However much an Aberdeen terrier may bear 'mid snow and ice a banner with the strange device Excelsior, he nearly always has to be content with dirty looks and the sharp, passionate bark.

Some minutes later my fellow rooster came out of the silence. No doubt the haughtiness of my manner had intimidated him, for there was a mildness in his voice which had not been there before.

"Mr. Wooster."

I turned coldly.

"Were you addressing me, Bassett?"

"There must be something we can do."

"You might fine the animal five pounds."

"We cannot stay here all night."

"Why not? What's to stop us?"

This held him. He relapsed into silence once more. And we were sitting there like a couple of Trappist monks when a voice said "Well, for heaven's sake!" and I perceived that Stiffy was with us.

Not surprising, of course, that she should have turned up sooner or later. If Scotties come, I ought to have said to myself, can Stiffy be far behind?

CHAPTER
NINE

CONSIDERING THAT so substantial a part of her waking hours is devoted to thrusting innocent bystanders into the soup, Stiffy is far prettier than she has any right to be. She's on the small side—petite, I believe, is the technical term—and I have always felt that when she and Stinker walk up the aisle together, if they ever do, their disparity in height should be good for a laugh or two from the ringside pews. The thought has occurred to me more than once that the correct response for Stinker to make, when asked by the M.C. if he is prepared to take this Stephanie to be his wedded wife, would be "Why, certainly, what there is of her."

"What on earth do you two think you're doing?" she inquired, not unnaturally surprised to see her uncle and an old friend in our current position. "And why have you been upsetting the furniture?"

"That was me," I said. "I bumped into the grandfather clock. I'm as bad as Stinker, aren't I, bumping into things, ha-ha."

"Less of the ha-ha," she riposted warmly. "And don't mention yourself in the same breath as my Harold. Well, that doesn't explain why you're sitting up there like a couple of buzzards on a treetop."

Pop Bassett intervened, speaking at his sniffiest. Her comparison of him to a buzzard, though perfectly accurate, seemed to have piqued him.

"We were savagely attacked by your dog."

"Not so much attacked," I said, "as given nasty looks. We didn't vouchsafe him time to attack us, deeming it best to get out of his sphere of influence before he could settle down to work. He's been trying to get at us for the last two hours; at least it seems like two hours."

She was quick to defend the dumb chum.

"Well, how can you blame the poor angel? Naturally he thought you were international spies in the pay of Moscow. Prowling about the house at this time of night. I can understand Bertie doing it, because he was dropped on the head as a baby, but I'm surprised at you, Uncle Watkyn. Why don't you go to bed?"

"I shall be delighted to go to bed," said Pop Bassett stiffly, "if you will remove this animal. He is a public menace."

"Very high-strung," I put in. "We were remarking on it only just now."

"He's all right, if you don't go out of your way to stir him up. Get back to your basket, Bartholomew, you bounder," said Stiffy, and such was the magic of her personality that the hound turned on its heel without a word and passed into the night.

Pop Bassett climbed down from the chest and directed a fishy magisterial look at me.

"Good night, Mr. Wooster. If there is any more of my furniture you wish to break, pray consider yourself at perfect liberty to indulge your peculiar tastes," he said, and he, too, passed into the night.

Stiffy looked after him with a thoughtful eye.

"I don't believe Uncle Watkyn likes you, Bertie. I noticed the way he kept staring at you at dinner, as if appalled. Well, I don't wonder your arrival hit him hard. It did me. I've never been so surprised in my life as when you suddenly bobbed up like a corpse rising to the surface of a sheet of water. Harold told me he had pleaded with you to come here but nothing would induce you. What made you change your mind?"

In my previous sojourn at Totleigh Towers circumstances had compelled me to confide in this young prune my position as regarded her cousin Madeline, so I had no hesitation now in giving her the lowdown.

"I learned that there was trouble between Madeline and Gussie, due, I have since been informed, to her forcing him to follow in the footsteps of the poet Shelley and become a vegetarian, and I felt that I might accomplish something as a *raisonneur*."

"As a whatonneur?"

"I thought that would be a bit above your head. It's a French expression meaning, I believe, though I would have to check with Jeeves, a calm kindly man of the world who intervenes when a rift has occurred between two loving hearts and brings them together again. Very essential in the present crisis."

[82]

"You mean that if Madeline hands Gussie the pink slip, she'll marry you?"

"That, broadly, is the strength of it. And while I admire and respect Madeline, I'm all against the idea of having her smiling face peeping at me over the coffeepot for the rest of my life. So I came here to see what I could do."

"Well, you couldn't have come at a better moment. Now you're here, you can get cracking on that job Harold told you I want you to do for me."

I saw that the time had come for some prompt in-the-bud-nipping.

"Include me out. I won't touch it. I know you and your jobs."

"But this is something quite simple. You can do it on your head. And you'll be bringing sunshine and happiness into the life of a poor slob who can do with a bit of both. Were you ever a Boy Scout?"

"Not since early boyhood."

"Then you've lots of leeway to make up in the way of kind deeds. This'll be a nice start for you. The facts are as follows."

"I don't want to hear them."

"You would prefer that I recalled Bartholomew and told him to go on where he left off?"

She had what Jeeves had called a talking point.

"Very well. Tell me all. But briefly."

"It won't take long, and then you can be off to beddy-bye. You remember that little black statuette thing on the table at dinner?"

"Ah yes, the eyesore."

"Uncle Watkyn bought it from a man called Plank."

"So I gathered."

"Well, do you know what he paid him for it?"

"A thousand quid, didn't you say?"

"No, I didn't. I said it was worth that. But he got it out of this poor blighter Plank for a fiver."

"You're kidding."

"No, I'm not. He paid him five pounds. He makes no secret of it. When we were at Brinkley, he was showing the thing to Mr. Travers and telling him all about it . . . how he happened to see it on Plank's mantelpiece and spotted how valuable it was and told Plank it was worth practically nothing but he would give him five pounds for it because he knew how hard up he was. He gloated over how clever he had been, and Mr. Travers writhed like an egg whisk."

I could well believe it. If there's one thing that makes a collector spit blood, it's hearing about another collector getting a bargain.

"How do you know Plank was hard up?"

"Well, would he have let the thing go for a fiver if he wasn't?"

"Something in that."

"You can't say Uncle Watkyn isn't a dirty dog."

"I would never dream of saying he isn't—and always has been—the dirtiest of dogs. It bears out what I have frequently maintained—that there are no depths to which magistrates won't stoop. I don't wonder you look askance. Your Uncle Watkyn stands revealed as a chiseler of the lowest type. But nothing to be done about it, of course."

"I don't know so much about that."

"Why, have you tried doing anything?"

"In a sort of way. I arranged that Harold should preach a very strong sermon on Naboth's Vineyard. Not that I suppose you've ever heard of Naboth's Vineyard."

I bridled. She had offended my amour-propre.

"I doubt if there's a man in London and the home counties who has the facts relating to Naboth's Vineyard more thoroughly at his fingertips than me. The news may not have reached you, but when at school I once won a prize for Scripture Knowledge."

"I bet you cheated."

"Not at all. Sheer merit. Did Stinker cooperate?"

"Yes, he thought it was a splendid idea and went about sucking throat pastilles for a week, so as to be in good voice. The setup was the same as the play in *Hamlet*. You know. With which to catch the conscience of the king and all that."

"Yes, I see the strategy all right. How did it work out?"

"It didn't. Harold lives in the cottage of Mrs. Bootle, the postman's wife, where they only have oil lamps, and the sermon was on a table with a lamp on it, and he bumped into the table and upset the lamp and it burned the sermon and he hadn't time to write it out again, so he had to dig out something on another topic from the old stockpile. He was terribly disappointed."

I pursed my lips, and was on the point of saying that of all the web-footed muddlers in existence H. P. Pinker took the well-known biscuit, when it occurred to me that it might possibly hurt her feelings, and I desisted. The last thing I wanted was to wound the child, particularly when I remembered that crack of hers about recalling Bartholomew.

"So we've got to handle the thing another way, and that's where you come in."

I smiled a tolerant smile.

"I can see where you're heading," I said. "You want me to go to your Uncle Watkyn and slip a jack under his better self. 'Play the game, Bassett,' you want me to say; 'let conscience be your guide, Bassett,' trying to drive it into his nut how wrong it is to put over a fast one on the widow and the orphan. I am assuming for purposes of argument that

[85]

Plank is an orphan, though possibly not a widow. But, my misguided young shrimp, do you really suppose that Pop Bassett looks on me as a friend and counselor to whom he is always willing to lend a ready ear? You yourself were stressing only a moment ago how allergic he was to the Wooster charm. It's no good me talking to him."

"I don't want you to."

"Then what do you want me to do?"

"I want you to pinch the thing and return it to Plank, who will then sell it to Mr. Travers at a proper price. The idea of Uncle Watkyn only giving him a fiver for it! We can't have him getting away with raw work like that. He needs a sharp lesson."

I smiled another tolerant smile. The young boll weevil amused me. I was thinking how right I had been in predicting that any job assigned by her to anyone would be unfit for human consumption.

"Well, really, Stiffy!"

The quiet rebuke in my voice ought to have bathed her in shame and remorse, but it didn't. She came back at me strongly.

"I don't know what you're Well-really-ing about. You're always pinching things, aren't you? Policemen's helmets and things like that."

I inclined the bean. It was true that I had once lived in Arcady.

"There is," I was obliged to concede, "a certain substance in what you say. I admit that in my time I may have removed a lid or two from the upper stories of members of the constabulary—"

"Well, then."

"—but only on Boat Race Night and when the heart was younger than it is as of even date. It was an episode of the sort that first brought me and your Uncle Watkyn together. But you can take it from me that the hot blood has cooled and I'm a reformed character. My answer to your suggestion is no."

"No?"

"N-ruddy-o," I said, making it clear to the meanest intelligence. "Why don't you pinch the thing yourself?"

"It wouldn't be any good. I couldn't take it to Plank. I'm confined to barracks. Bartholomew bit the butler, and the sins of the Scotty are visited upon its owner. I do think you might reconsider, Bertie."

"Not a hope."

"You're a blighter!"

"But a blighter who knows his own mind and is not to be shaken by argument or plea, however specious."

She was silent for a space. Then she gave a little sigh.

"Oh, dear," she said. "And I did hope I wouldn't have to tell Madeline about Gussie."

I gave another of those visible starts of mine. I've seldom heard words I liked the sound of less. Fraught with sinister significance they seemed to me.

"Do you know what happened tonight, Bertie? I was roused from sleep about an hour ago, and what do you think roused me? Stealthy footsteps, no less. I crept out of my room, and I saw Gussie sneaking down the stairs. All was darkness, of course, but he had a little torch and it shone on his spectacles. I followed him. He went to the kitchen. I peered in, and there was the cook shoveling cold steak and kidney pie into him like a stevedore loading a grain ship. And the thought flashed into my mind that if Madeline heard of this, she would give him the bum's rush before he knew what had hit him."

"But a girl doesn't give a fellow the bum's rush just because she's told him to stick to the sprouts and spinach and she hears that he's been wading into the steak and kidney pie," I said, trying to reassure myself but not getting within several yards of it.

"I bet Madeline would."

And so, thinking it over, did I. You can't judge goofs like Madeline Bassett by ordinary standards. What the normal popsy would do and what she would do in any given circumstances were two distinct and separate things. I had not forgotten the time when she had severed relations with Gussie purely because through no fault of his own he got stinko when about to present the prizes at Market Snodsbury Grammar School.

"You know how high her ideals are. Yes, sir, if someone were to drop an incautious word to her about tonight's orgy, those wedding bells would not ring out. Gussie would be at liberty, and she would start looking about her for somebody else to fill the vacant spot. I really think you'll have to reconsider that decision of yours, Bertie, and do just this one more bit of pinching."

"Oh, my sainted aunt!"

I spoke as harts do when heated in the chase and panting for cooling streams. It would have been plain to a far less astute mind than mine that this blighted Byng had got me by the short hairs and was in a position to dictate tactics and strategy.

Blackmail, of course, but the gentler sex loves blackmail. Not once but on several occasions has my aunt Dahlia bent me to her will by threatening that if I didn't play ball she would bar me from her table, thus dashing Anatole's lunches and dinners from my lips. Show me a delicately nurtured female, and I will show you a ruthless Napoleon of Crime prepared without turning a hair to put the screws on some unfortunate male whose services she happens to be in need of. There ought to be a law.

"It looks as if the die were cast," I said reluctantly.

"It is," she assured me.

"You're really adamant?"

"Couldn't be more so. My heart bleeds for Plank, and I'm going to see that justice is done."

"Right ho, then. I'll have a crack at it."

"That's my little man. The whole thing's so frightfully easy and simple. All you have to do is lift the thing off the dining-room table and smuggle it over to Plank. Think how his face'll light up when you walk in on him with it. 'My hero!' I expect he'll say."

And with a laugh which, though silvery, grated on my ear like a squeaking slate pencil she buzzed off.

CHAPTER
TEN

PROCEEDING TO my room and turning in between the sheets,
I composed myself for sleep, but I didn't get a lot of it and
what I did get was much disturbed by dreams of being
chased across difficult country by sharks, some of them looking like Stiffy, some like Sir Watkyn Bassett, others like the
dog Bartholomew. When Jeeves came shimmering in next
morning with the breakfast tray, I lost no time in supplying
him with full information *re* the harrow I found myself the
toad under.

"You see the posish, Jeeves," I concluded. "When the
loss of the thing is discovered and the hue and cry sets in,
who will be the immediate suspect? Wooster, Bertram. My
name in this house is already mud, and the men up top will
never think of looking further for the guilty party. On the

other hand, if I refuse to sit in, Stiffy will consider herself scorned, and we all know what happens when you scorn a woman. She'll tell Madeline Bassett that Gussie has been at the steak and kidney pie, and ruin and desolation will ensue. I see no way of beating the game."

To my surprise, instead of raising an eyebrow the customary eighth of an inch and saying "Most disturbing, sir," he came within an ace of smiling. That is to say, the left corner of his mouth quivered almost imperceptibly before returning to position one.

"You cannot accede to Miss Byng's request, sir."

I took an astonished sip of coffee. I couldn't follow his train of thought. It seemed to me that he couldn't have been listening.

"But if I don't, she'll squeal to the FBI."

"No, sir, for the lady will be forced to admit that it is physically impossible for you to carry out her wishes. The statuette is no longer at large. It has been placed in Sir Watkyn's collection room behind a stout steel door."

"Good Lord! How do you know?"

"I chanced to pass the dining room, sir, and inadvertently overheard a conversation between Sir Watkyn and his lordship."

"Call him Spode."

"Very good, sir. Mr. Spode was observing to Sir Watkyn that he had not at all liked the interest you displayed in the figurine at dinner last night."

"I was just giving Pop B the old salve in the hope of sweetening the atmosphere a bit."

"Precisely, sir, but your statement that the object was 'just the sort of thing Uncle Tom would like to have' made a deep impression on Mr. Spode. Remembering the unfortunate episode of the cow creamer, which did so much to mar the pleasantness of your previous visit to Totleigh Towers, he informed Sir Watkyn that he had revised his original view that you were here to attempt to lure Miss Bassett from Mr. Fink-Nottle, and that he was now convinced that your motive in coming to the house had to do with the figurine, and that you were planning to purloin it on Mr. Travers' behalf. Sir Watkyn, who appeared much moved, accepted the theory in toto, all the more readily because of an encounter which he said he had had with you in the early hours of this morning."

I nodded.

"Yes, we got together in the hall at, I suppose, about one A.M. I had gone down to see if I could get a bit of that steak and kidney pie."

"I quite understand, sir. It was an injudicious thing to do, if I may say so, but the claims of steak and kidney pie are of course paramount. It was immediately after this that Sir Watkyn fell in with Mr. Spode's suggestion that the statuette be placed under lock and key in the collection room. I presume that it is now there, and when it is explained to Miss Byng that only by means of burglars' tools or a flask of trinitrotoluol could you obtain access to it and that neither of these is in your possession, I am sure the lady will see reason and recede from her position."

Only the circumstance of my being in bed at the moment kept me from dancing a few carefree steps.

"You speak absolute sooth, Jeeves. This lets me out."

"Completely, sir."

"Perhaps you wouldn't mind going and explaining the position of affairs to Stiffy now. You can tell the story so much better than I could, and she ought to be given the lowdown as soon as possible. I don't know where she is at this time of day, but you'll find her messing about somewhere, I've no doubt."

"I saw Miss Byng in the garden with Mr. Pinker, sir. I think she was trying to prepare him for his approaching ordeal."

"Eh?"

"If you recall, sir, owing to the temporary indisposition of the vicar, Mr. Pinker will be in sole charge of the school treat tomorrow, and he views the prospect with not unnatural qualms. There is a somewhat lawless element among the schoolchildren of Totleigh-in-the-Wold, and he fears the worst."

"Well, tell Stiffy to take a couple of minutes off from the pep talk and listen to your communiqué."

"Very good, sir."

He was absent quite a time—so long, in fact, that I was dressed when he returned.

"I saw Miss Byng, sir."

"And—"

"She is still insistent that you restore the statuette to Mr. Plank."

"She's cuckoo. I can't get into the collection room."

"No, sir, but Miss Byng can. She informs me that not long ago Sir Watkyn chanced to drop his key, and she picked it up and omitted to apprise him. Sir Watkyn had another key made, but the original remains in Miss Byng's possession."

I clutched the brow.

"You mean she can get into the room any time she feels like it?"

"Precisely, sir. Indeed, she has just done so."

And so saying he fished the eyesore from an inner pocket and handed it to me.

"Miss Byng suggests that you take the object to Mr.

Plank after luncheon. In her droll way she said the meal—I quote her words—would put the necessary stuffing into you and nerve you for the . . . It is somewhat early, sir, but shall I get you a little brandy?"

"Not a little, Jeeves," I said. "Fetch the cask."

I don't know how Emerald Stoker was with brush and palette, never having seen any of her output, but she unquestionably had what it takes where cooking was concerned, and any householder would have been glad to sign her up for the duration. The lunch she provided was excellent, everything most toothsome.

But with this ghastly commission of Stiffy's on the agenda paper, I had little appetite for her offerings. The brow was furrowed, the manner distrait, the stomach full of butterflies.

"Jeeves," I said as he accompanied me to my car at the conclusion of the meal, speaking rather peevishly, perhaps, for I was not my usual sunny self, "doesn't it strike you as odd that, with infant mortality so rife, a girl like Stiffy should have been permitted to survive into the early twenties? Some mismanagement there. What's the tree I read about somewhere that does you in if you sit under it?"

"The upas tree, sir."

"She's a female upas tree. It's not safe to come near her. Disaster on every side is what she strews. And another thing. It's all very well for her to say . . . glibly?"

"Or airily, sir. The words are synonymous."

"It's all very well for her to say glibly or airily, 'Take this blasted eyesore to Plank,' but how do I find him? I can't go rapping on every door in Hockley-cum-Meston, saying, 'Excuse me, are you Plank?' It'd be like looking for a needle in a haystack."

"A very colorful image, sir. I appreciate your difficulty.

I would suggest that you proceed to the local post office and institute inquiries there. Post-office officials invariably have information at their disposal as to the whereabouts of dwellers in the vicinity."

He had not erred. Braking the car in the Hockley-cum-Meston High Street, I found that the post office was one of those shops you get in villages, where, in addition to enjoying the postal facilities, you can purchase cigarettes, pipe tobacco, wool, lollipops, string, socks, boots, overalls, picture postcards, and bottles containing yellow nonalcoholic drinks, probably fizzy. In answer to my query, the old lady behind the counter told me I would find Plank up at the big house with the red shutters about half a mile further back along the road. She seemed a bit disappointed that information was all I was after and that I had no intention of buying a pair of socks or a ball of string, but she bore up philosophically, and I toddled back to the car.

I remembered the house she had spoken of, having passed it on my way. Imposing mansion with a lot of land. This Plank, I took it, would be some sort of laborer on the estate. I pictured him as a sturdy, gnarled old fellow whose sailor son had brought home the eyesore from one of his voyages, and neither of them had had the foggiest that it was valuable. "I'll put it on the mantelpiece, Dad," no doubt the son had said. "It'll look well up there." To which the old gaffer had replied, "Aye, lad, gormed if 'twon't look gradely on the mantelpiece." Or words to that effect. I can't do the dialect, of course. So they had shoved it on the mantelpiece, and then along had come Sir Watkyn Bassett with his smooth city ways and made suckers out of parent and offspring. Happening all the time, that sort of thing.

I reached the house and was about to knock on the door

when there came bustling up an elderly gentleman with a square face, much tanned, as if he had been sitting out in the sun quite a lot without his parasol.

"Oh, there you are," he said. "Hope I haven't kept you waiting. We were having football practice, and I lost track of the time. Come in, my dear fellow, come in."

I need scarcely say that this exuberant welcome to one who, whatever his merits, was a total stranger warmed my heart quite a good deal. It was with the feeling that his attitude did credit to Gloucestershire hospitality that I followed him through a hall liberally besprinkled with the heads of lions, leopards, gnus, and other fauna into a room with French windows opening on the front garden. Here he left me while he went off to fetch drinks, his first question having been, Would I care for one for the tonsils, to which I had replied with considerable enthusiasm that I would. When he returned, he found me examining the photographs on the wall. The one on which my eye was resting at the moment was a school football group, and it was not difficult to spot the identity of the juvenile delinquent holding the ball and sitting in the middle.

"You?" I said.

"That's me," he replied. "My last year at school. I skippered the side that season. That's old Scrubby Willoughby sitting next to me. Fast-wing three-quarter, but never would learn to give the reverse pass."

"He wouldn't?" I said, shocked. I hadn't the remotest what he was talking about, but he had said enough to show me that this Willoughby must have been a pretty dubious character, and when he went on to tell me that poor old Scrubby had died of cirrhosis of the liver in the Federal

Malay States, I wasn't really surprised. I imagine these fellows who won't learn to give the reverse pass generally come to a fairly sticky end.

"Chap on my other side is Smiler Todd, prop forward."

"Prop forward, eh?"

"And a very good one. Played for Cambridge later on. You fond of Rugger?"

"I don't think I know him."

"Rugby football."

"Oh, ah. No, I've never gone in for it."

"You haven't?"

"No."

"Good God!"

I could see that I had sunk pretty low in his estimation, but he was a host and managed to fight down the feeling of nausea with which my confession had afflicted him.

"I've always been mad keen on Rugger. Didn't get much of it after leaving school, as they stationed me in West Africa. Tried to teach the natives there the game, but had to give it up. Too many deaths, with the inevitable subsequent blood feuds. Retired now and settled down here. I'm trying to make Hockley-cum-Meston the best football village in these parts, and I will say for the lads that they're coming on nicely. What we need is a good prop forward, and I can't find one. But you don't want to hear all this. You want to know about my Brazilian expedition."

"Oh, have you been to Brazil?"

I seemed to have said the wrong thing, as one so often does. He stared.

"Didn't you know I'd been to Brazil?"

"Nobody tells me anything."

"I should have thought they'd have briefed you at the

office. Seems silly to send a reporter all the way down here without telling him what they're sending him for."

I'm pretty astute, and I saw there had been a mix-up somewhere.

"Were you expecting a reporter?"

"Of course I was. Aren't you from the *Daily Express*?"

"Sorry, no."

"I thought you must be the chap who was coming to interview me about my Brazilian explorations."

"Oh, you're an explorer?"

Again I had said the wrong thing. He was plainly piqued.

"What did you think I was? Does the name Plank mean nothing to you?"

"Is your name Plank?"

"Of course it is."

"Well, what a very odd coincidence," I said, intrigued. "I'm looking for a character called Plank. Not you, some-body else. The bimbo I want is a sturdy tiller of the soil, probably gnarled, with a sailor son. As you have the same name as him, you'll probably be interested in the story I'm about to relate. I have here," I said, producing the black amber thing, "a whatnot."

He gaped at it.

"Where did you get that? That's the bit of native sculpture I picked up on the Congo and sold to Sir Watkyn Bassett."

I was amazed.

"*You* sold it to him?"

"Certainly."

"Well, shiver my timbers!"

I was conscious of a Boy Scoutful glow. I liked this Plank, and I rejoiced that it was in my power to do him as good a turn as anyone had ever done anybody. God bless Bertram Wooster, I felt he'd be saying in another couple of ticks. For the first time I was glad that Stiffy had sent me on this mission.

"Then I'll tell you what," I said. "If you'll just give me five pounds—"

I broke off. He was looking at me with a cold, glassy stare, as no doubt he had looked at the late lions, leopards, and gnus whose remains were to be viewed on the walls of the outer hall. Fellows at the Drones who have tried to touch Oofy Prosser, the club millionaire, for a trifle to see them through till next Wednesday have described him to me as looking just like that.

"Oh, so that's it!" he said, and even Pop Bassett could not have spoken more nastily. "I've got your number now. I've met your sort all over the world. You won't get any five pounds, my man. You sit where you are and don't move. I'm going to call the police."

"It will not be necessary, sir," said a respectful voice, and Jeeves entered through the French window.

CHAPTER
ELEVEN

HIS ADVENT drew from me a startled goggle and, I rather think, a cry of amazement. Last man I'd expected to see, and how he had got here defeated me. I've sometimes felt that he must dematerialize himself like those fellows in India—fakirs, I think they're called—who fade into thin air in Bombay and turn up five minutes later in Calcutta or points west with all the parts reassembled.

Nor could I see how he had divined that the young master was in sore straits and in urgent need of his assistance, unless it was all done by what I believe is termed telepathy. Still, here he was, with his head bulging at the back and on his face that look of quiet intelligence which comes from eating lots of fish, and I welcomed his presence. I knew from experience what a wizard he was at removing the oppressed from the soup, and the soup was what I was at this point in my affairs deeply immersed in.

"Major Plank?" he said.

Plank, too, was goggling.

"Who on earth are you?"

"Chief Inspector Witherspoon, sir, of Scotland Yard. Has this man been attempting to obtain money from you?"

"Just been doing that very thing."

"As I suspected. We have had our eye on him for a long time but till now have never been able to apprehend him in the act."

"Notorious crook, is he?"

"Precisely, sir. He is a confidence man of considerable eminence in the underworld who makes a practice of calling at houses and extracting money from their owners with some plausible story."

"He does more than that. He pinches things from people and tries to sell them. Look at that statuette he's holding. It's a thing I sold to Sir Watkyn Bassett, who lives at Totleigh-in-the-Wold, and he had the cool cheek to come here and try to sell it to me for five pounds."

"Indeed, sir? With your permission I will impound the object."

"You'll need it as evidence?"

"Exactly, sir. I shall now take him to Totleigh Towers and confront him with Sir Watkyn."

"Yes, do. That'll teach him. Nasty hangdog look the fellow's got. I suspected from the first he was wanted by the police. Had him under observation for a long time, have you?"

"For a very long time, sir. He is known to us at the Yard as Alpine Joe, because he always wears an Alpine hat."

"He's got it with him now."

"He never moves without it."

"You'd think he'd have the sense to adopt some rude disguise."

"You would indeed, sir, but the mental processes of a man like that are hard to follow."

"Then there's no need for me to phone the local police?"

"None, sir. I will take him into custody."

"You wouldn't like me to hit him over the head first with a Zulu knobkerrie?"

"Unnecessary, sir."

"It might be safer."

"No, sir, I am sure he will come quietly."

"Well, have it your own way. But don't let him give you the slip."

"I will be very careful, sir."

"And shove him into a dungeon with dripping walls and see to it that he is well gnawed by rats."

"Very good, sir."

What with all the stuff about reverse passes and prop forwards, plus the strain of seeing gentlemen's personal gentlemen appear from nowhere and of having to listen to that loose talk about Zulu knobkerries, the Wooster bean was not at its best as we moved off, and there was nothing in the way of conversational give-and-take until we had reached my car, which I had left at the front gate.

"Chief Inspector *who?*" I said, recovering a modicum of speech as we arrived at our objective.

"Witherspoon, sir."

"Why Witherspoon? On the other hand," I added, for I like to look on both sides of a thing, "why not Witherspoon? However, that is not germane to the issue and can be reserved for discussion later. The real point—the nub—the thing that should be threshed out immediately—is how on earth do you come to be here?"

"I anticipated that my arrival might occasion you a certain surprise, sir. I hastened after you directly I learned of the revelation Sir Watkyn had made to Miss Byng, for I foresaw that your interview with Major Plank would be embarrassing, and I hoped to be able to intercept you before you could establish communication with him."

Practically all of this floated past me.

"How do you mean, the revelation Pop Bassett made to Stiffy?"

"It occurred shortly after luncheon, sir. Miss Byng informs me that she decided to approach Sir Watkyn and make a last appeal to his better feelings. As you are aware, the matter of the statuette has always been one that affected her deeply. She thought that if she reproached Sir Watkyn with sufficient vehemence, something constructive might result. Greatly to her astonishment, she had hardly begun to speak when Sir Watkyn, chuckling heartily, asked her if she could keep a secret. He then revealed that there was no foundation for the story he had told Mr. Travers and that in actual fact he had paid Major Plank a thousand pounds for the object."

It took me perhaps a quarter of a minute to sort all this out.

"A thousand quid?"

"Yes, sir."

"Not a fiver?"

"No, sir."

"You mean he lied to Uncle Tom?"

"Yes, sir."

"What on earth did he do that for?"

[103]

I thought he would say he hadn't a notion, but he didn't.

"I think Sir Watkyn's motive was obvious, sir."

"Not to me."

"He acted from a desire to exasperate Mr. Travers. Mr. Travers is a collector, and collectors are never pleased when they learn that a rival collector has acquired at an insignificant price an objet d'art of great value."

It penetrated. I saw what he meant. The discovery that Pop Bassett had got hold of a thousand-quid thingummy for practically nothing would have been gall and w. to Uncle Tom. Stiffy had described him as writhing like an egg whisk, and I could well believe it. It must have been agony for the poor old buster.

"You've hit it, Jeeves. It's just what Pop Bassett would do. Nothing would please him better than to spoil Uncle Tom's day. What a man, Jeeves!"

"Yes, sir."

"Would you like to have a mind like his?"

"No, sir."

"Nor me. It just shows how being a magistrate saps the moral fiber. I remember thinking as I stood before him in the dock that he had a shifty eye and that I wouldn't trust him as far as I could throw an elephant. I suppose all magistrates are like that."

"There may be exceptions, sir."

"I doubt it. Twisters, every one of them. So my errand was . . . what, Jeeves?"

"Bootless, sir."

"Bootless? It doesn't sound right, but I suppose you know. Well, I wish the news you've just sprung could have broken before I presented myself chez Plank. I would have been spared a testing ordeal."

"I can appreciate the nervous strain you must have undergone, sir. It is unfortunate that I was not able to arrive earlier."

"How did you arrive at all? That's what's puzzling me. You can't have walked."

"No, sir. I borrowed Miss Byng's car. I left it some little distance down the road and proceeded to the house on foot. Hearing voices, I approached the French window and listened and was thus enabled to intervene at the crucial moment."

"Very resourceful."

"Thank you, sir."

"I should like to express my gratitude. And when I say gratitude, I mean heartfelt gratitude."

"Not at all, sir. It was a pleasure."

"But for you, Plank would have had me in the local calaboose in a matter of minutes. Who is he, by the way? I got the impression that he was an explorer of sorts."

"Yes, sir."

"Pretty far-flung, I gathered."

"Extremely, sir. He has recently returned from an expedition into the interior of Brazil. He inherited the house where he resides from a deceased godfather. He breeds cocker spaniels, suffers somewhat from malaria, and eats only nonfattening protein bread."

"You seem to have got him taped all right."

"I made inquiries at the post office, sir. The person behind the counter was most informative. I also learned that Major Plank is an enthusiast on Rugby football and is hoping to make Hockley-cum-Meston invincible on the field."

"Yes, so he was telling me. You aren't a prop forward, are you, Jeeves?"

"No, sir. Indeed, I do not know what the term signifies."

"I don't, either, except that it's something a team has to have if it's hoping to do down the opposition at Rugby football. Plank, I believe, has searched high and low for one, but his errand has been bootless. Rather sad, when you come to think of it. All that money, all those cocker spaniels, all that protein bread, but no prop forward. Still, that's life."

"Yes indeed, sir."

I slid behind the steering wheel and told him to hop in.

"But I was forgetting. You've got Stiffy's car. Then I'll be driving on. The sooner I get this statuette thing back into her custody, the better."

He didn't shake his head, because he never shakes his head, but he raised the southeast corner of a warning eyebrow.

"If you will pardon the suggestion, sir, I think it would be more advisable for me to take the object to Miss Byng. It would scarcely be prudent for you to enter the environs of Totleigh Towers with it on your person. You might encounter his lordship . . . I should say Mr. Spode."

I Well-I'll-be-dashed. He had surprised me.

"Surely you aren't suggesting that he would frisk me?"

"I think it highly possible, sir. In the conversation which I overheard, Mr. Spode gave me the impression of being prepared to stop at nothing. If you will give me the object, I will see that Miss Byng restores it to the collection room at the earliest possible moment.

I mused, but not for long. I was only too pleased to get rid of the beastly thing.

"Very well, if you say so. Here you are. Though I think you're wronging Spode."

"I think not, sir."

And blow me tight if he wasn't right. Scarcely had I

steered the car into the stable yard when a solid body darkened the horizon, and there was Spode, looking like Chief Inspector Witherspoon about to make a pinch.

"Wooster!" he said.

"Speaking," I said.

"Get out of that car," he said. "I'm going to search it."

CHAPTER
TWELVE

I was conscious of a thrill of thankfulness for Jeeves' prescience, if prescience is the word I want. I mean that uncanny knack he has of peering into the future and forming his plans and schemes well ahead of time. But for his thoughtful diagnosis of the perils that lay before me, I should at this juncture have been deep in the mulligatawny and no hope of striking for the shore. As it was, I was able to be nonchalant, insouciant, and debonair. I was like the fellow I once heard Jeeves speak of who was armed so strong in honesty that somebody's threats passed by him as the idle wind, which he respected not. I think if Spode had been about three feet shorter and not so wide across the shoulders, I would have laughed a mocking laugh and quite possibly have flicked my cambric handkerchief in his face.

He was eyeing me piercingly, little knowing what an ass he was going to feel before yonder sun had set.

"I have just searched your room."

"You have? You surprise me. Looking for something, were you?"

"You know what I'm looking for. That amber statuette you said your uncle would be so glad to have."

"Oh, that? I understood it was in the collection room."

"Who told you that?"

"A usually well-informed source."

"Well, it is no longer in the collection room. Somebody has removed it."

"Most extraordinary."

"And when I say 'somebody,' I mean a slimy sneak thief of the name of Wooster. The thing isn't in your bedroom, so if it is not in your car, you must have it on you. Turn out your pockets."

I humored his request, largely influenced by the fact that there was so much of him. A Singer midget would have found me far less obliging. The contents having been placed before him, he snorted in a disappointed way, as if he had hoped for better things, and dived into the car, opening drawers and looking under cushions. And Stiffy, coming along at this moment, drank in his vast trouser seat with a curious eye.

"What goes on?" she asked.

This time I did laugh that mocking laugh. It seemed to be indicated.

"You know that black eyesore thing that was on the dinner table? Apparently it's disappeared, and Spode has got the extraordinary idea that I've pinched it and am holding it . . . what's the word . . . not incognito . . . incommunicado, that's it. He thinks I'm holding it incommunicado."

"He does?"

"So he says."

"Man must be an ass."

Spode wheeled around, flushed with his excesses. I was pleased to see that while looking under the seat he had got a bit of oil on his nose. He eyed Stiffy bleakly.

"Did you call me an ass?"

"Certainly I did. I was taught by a long series of governesses always to speak the truth. The idea of accusing Bertie of taking that statuette."

"It does sound silly," I agreed. "Bizarre is perhaps the word."

"The thing's in Uncle Watkyn's collection room."

"It is not in the collection room."

"Who says so?"

"I say so."

"Well, I say it is. Go and look, if you don't believe me. Stop that, Bartholomew, you blighted dog!" bellowed Stiffy, abruptly changing the subject, and she hastened off on winged feet to confer with the hound, who had found something in, I presumed, the last stages of decay and was rolling on it. I could follow her train of thought. Scotties at their best are niffy. Add to their natural bouquet the aroma of a dead rat or whatever it was, and you have a mixture too rich for the human nostril. There was a momentary altercation, and Bartholomew, cursing a good deal, as was natural, was hauled off tubwards.

A minute or two later Spode returned with most of the stuffing removed from his person.

"I seem to have done you an injustice, Wooster," he said, and I was amazed that he had it in him to speak so meekly.

The Woosters are always magnanimous. We do not crush the vanquished beneath the iron heel.

"Oh, was the thing there all right?"

"Er—yes. Yes, it was."

"Ah well, we all make mistakes."

"I could have sworn it had gone."

"But wasn't the door locked?"

"Yes."

"Reminds you of one of those mystery stories, doesn't it, where there's a locked room with no windows, and blowed if one fine morning you don't find a millionaire inside with a dagger of Oriental design sticking in his wishbone. You've got some oil on your nose."

"Oh, have I?" he said, feeling.

"Now you've got it on your cheek. I'd go and join Bartholomew in the bathtub if I were you."

"I will. Thank you, Wooster."

"Not at all, Spode, or, rather, Sidcup. Don't spare the soap."

I suppose there's nothing that braces one more thoroughly than the spectacle of the forces of darkness stubbing their toe, and the heart was light as I made my way to the house. What with this and what with that, it was as though a great weight had rolled off me. Birds sang, insects buzzed, and I felt that what they were trying to say was "All is well. Bertram has come through."

But a thing I've often noticed is that when I've got something off my mind, it pretty nearly always happens that Fate sidles up and shoves on something else, as if curious to see how much the traffic will bear. It went into its act on the present occasion. Feeling that I needed something else to worry about, it spat on its hands and got down to

[111]

it, allowing Madeline Bassett to corner me as I was passing through the hall.

Even if she had been her normal soupy self, she would have been the last person I wanted to have a word with, but this she was far from being. Something had happened to remove the droopiness, and her eyes had a gleam in them which filled me with a nameless fear. She was obviously all steamed up for some reason, and it was plain that what she was about to say was not going to make the last of the Woosters clap his hands in glee and start chanting hosannas like the Cherubim and Seraphim, if I've got the names right. A moment later she revealed what it was that was eating her, dishing it out without what I believe is called preamble.

"I am furious with Augustus!" she said, and my heart stood still. It was as if the Totleigh Towers specter, if there was one, had laid an icy hand on it.

"Why, what's happened?"

"He was very rude to Roderick."

This seemed incredible. Nobody but an all-in wrestling champion would be rude to a fellow as big as Spode.

"Surely not?"

"I mean he was very rude *about* Roderick. He said he was sick and tired of seeing him clumping about the place as if it belonged to him, and hadn't he got a home of his own, and if Daddy had an ounce more sense than a billiard ball he would charge him rent. He was most offensive."

My h. stood stiller. It is not stretching the facts to say that I was appalled and all of a doodah. It just showed, I was telling myself, what a vegetarian diet can do to a chap, changing him in a flash from a soft-boiled to a hard-boiled egg. I have no doubt the poet Shelley's circle noticed the same thing with the poet Shelley.

I tried to pour oil on the troubled w's.

"Probably just kidding, don't you think?"

"No, I don't."

"He didn't say it with a twinkle in his eye?"

"No."

"Nor with a light laugh?"

"No."

"You might not have noticed it. Very easy to miss, these light laughs."

"He meant every word he said."

"Then it was probably just a momentary spasm of what-d'you-call-it. Irritability. We all have them."

She ground a tooth or two. At least, it looked as if that was what she was doing.

"It was nothing of the kind. He was harsh and bitter, and he has been like that for a long time. I noticed it first at Brinkley. One morning we had walked in the meadows and the grass was all covered with little wreaths of mist, and I said, Didn't he sometimes feel that they were the elves' bridal veils, and he said sharply, 'No, never,' adding that he had never heard such a silly idea in his life."

Well, of course, he was perfectly correct, but it was no good pointing that out to a girl like Madeline Bassett.

"And that evening we were watching the sunset, and I said sunsets always made me think of the Blessed Damozel leaning out from the gold bar of heaven, and he said, 'Who?' and I said, 'The Blessed Damozel,' and he said, 'Never heard of her.' And he said that sunsets made him sick and so did the Blessed Damozel and he had a pain in his inside."

I saw that the time had come to be a *raisonneur*.

"This was at Brinkley?"

"Yes."

"I see. After you had made him become a vegetarian. Are you sure," I said, raisonneuring like nobody's business,

[113]

"that you were altogether wise in confining him to spinach and what not? Many a proud spirit rebels when warned off the proteins. And I don't know if you know it, but medical research has established that the ideal diet is one in which animal and vegetable foods are balanced. It's something to do with the something acids required by the body."

I won't say she actually snorted, but the sound she uttered was certainly on the border line of the snort.

"What nonsense!"

"It's what doctors say."

"Which doctors?"

"Well-known Harley Street physicians."

"I don't believe it. Thousands of people are vegetarians and enjoy perfect health."

"Bodily health, yes," I said, cleverly seizing on the debating point. "But what of the soul? If you suddenly steer a fellow off the steaks and chops, it does something to his soul. My Aunt Agatha once made my Uncle Percy be a vegetarian, and his whole nature became soured. Not," I was forced to admit, "that it wasn't fairly soured already, as anyone's would be who was in constant contact with my Aunt Agatha. I bet you'll find that that's all that's wrong with Gussie. He simply wants a mutton chop or two under his belt."

"Well, he's not going to have them. And if he continues to behave like a sulky child, I shall know what to do about it."

I remember Stinker Pinker telling me once that toward the end of his time at Oxford he was down in Bethnel Green spreading the light and a costermonger kicked him in the stomach. He said it gave him a strange, confused, dreamlike feeling, and that's what these ominous words of M. Bassett's gave me now. She had spoken them from between teeth which, if not actually clenched, were the next thing to it, and it was as if the substantial boot of a vendor of blood oranges and bananas had caught me squarely in the solar plexus.

"Er—what will you do about it?"

"Never mind."

I put out a cautious feeler.

"Suppose . . . not that it's likely to happen, of course . . . but suppose Gussie, maddened by abstinence, were to go off and tuck into . . . well, to take an instance at random, cold steak and kidney pie, what would be the upshot?"

I had never supposed that she had it in her to give anyone a piercing look, but that is what she gave me now. I don't think even Aunt Agatha's eyes have bored more deeply into me.

"Are you telling me, Bertie, that Augustus has been eating steak and kidney pie?"

"Good heavens, no. It was just a thingummy."

"I don't understand you."

"What do they call questions that aren't really questions? Begins with an h. Hypothetical, that's the word. It was just a hypothetical question."

"Oh? Well, the answer to it is that if I found that Augustus had been eating the flesh of animals slain in anger, I would have nothing more to do with him," she said, and she biffed off, leaving me a spent force and a mere shell of my former self.

CHAPTER
THIRTEEN

THE FOLLOWING day dawned bright and fair. At least I suppose it did. I didn't see it dawning myself, having dropped off into a troubled slumber some hours before it got its nose down to it, but when the mists of sleep cleared and I was able to attend to what was going on, sunshine was seeping through the window and the ear detected the chirping of about seven hundred and fifty birds, not one of whom, unlike me, appeared to have a damn thing on his or her mind. As carefree a bunch as I've ever struck, and it gave me the pip to listen to them, for melancholy had marked me for her own, as the fellow said, and all this buck and heartiness simply stepped up the gloom in which my yesterday's chat with Madeline Bassett had plunged me.

As may well be imagined, her obiter dicta, as I believe they're called, had got right in amongst me. This, it was plain, was no mere lovers' tiff, to be cleaned up with a couple of tears and a kiss or two, but a real Class A rift which, if prompt steps were not taken through the proper channels, would put the lute right out of business and make it as mute as a drum with a hole in it. And the problem of how those steps were to be taken defeated me. Two iron wills had clashed. On the one hand we had Madeline's strong anti-flesh-food bias, on the other Gussie's firm determination to get all the cuts off the joint that were coming to him. What, I asked myself, would the harvest be, and I was still shuddering at the thought of what the future might hold when Jeeves trickled in with the morning cup of tea.

"Eh?" I said absently as he put it on the table. Usually I spring at the refreshing fluid like a seal going after a slice of fish. Preoccupied, if you know what I mean. Or distrait, if you care to put it that way.

"I was saying that we are fortunate in having a fine day for the school treat, sir."

I sat up with a jerk, upsetting the cuppa as deftly as if I'd been the Rev. H. P. Pinker.

"Is it today?"

"This afternoon, sir."

I groaned one of those hollow ones.

"It needed but this, Jeeves."

"Sir?"

"The last straw. I'd enough on my mind already."

"There is something disturbing you, sir?"

"You're right there is. Hell's foundations are quivering. What do you call it when a couple of nations start off by being all palsy-walsy and then begin calling each other ticks and bounders?"

"Relations have deteriorated would be the customary phrase, sir."

"Well, relations have deteriorated between Miss Bassett

and Gussie. He, as we know, was already disgruntled, and now she's disgruntled, too. She has taken exception to a derogatory crack he made about the sunset. She thinks highly of sunsets, and he told her they made him sick. Can you believe this?"

"Quite readily, sir. Mr. Fink-Nottle was commenting to me on the sunset yesterday evening. He said it looked so like a slice of underdone beef that it tortured him to see it. One can appreciate his feelings."

"I dare say, but I wish he'd keep them to himself. He also appears to have spoken disrespectfully of the Blessed Damozel. Who's the Blessed Damozel, Jeeves? I don't seem to have heard of her."

"The heroine of a poem by the late Dante Gabriel Rossetti, sir. She leaned out from the gold bar of heaven."

"Yes, I gathered that. That much was specified."

"Her eyes were deeper than the depths of waters stilled at even. She had three lilies in her hand, and the stars in her hair were seven."

"Oh, were they? Well, be that as it may, Gussie said she made him sick, too, and Miss Bassett's as sore as a sunburned neck."

"Most disturbing, sir."

"Disturbing is the word. If things go on the way they are, no bookie would give odds of less than a hundred to eight on this betrothal lasting another week. I've seen betrothals in my time, many of them, but never one that looked more likely to come apart at the seams than that of Augustus Fink-Nottle and Madeline, daughter of Sir Watkyn and the late Lady Bassett. The suspense is awful. Who was the chap I remember reading about somewhere, who had a sword hanging over him attached to a single hair?"

"Damocles, sir. It is an old Greek legend."

"Well, I know just how he must have felt. And with this on my mind, I'm expected to attend a ruddy school treat. I won't go."

"Your absence may cause remark, sir."

"I don't care. They won't get a smell of me. I'm oiling out, and let them make of it what they will."

Apart from anything else, I was remembering the story I had heard Pongo Twistleton tell one night at the Drones, illustrative of how unbridled passions are apt to become at these binges. Pongo got mixed up once in a school treat down in Somersetshire, and his description of how in order to promote a game called "Is Mr. Smith at Home?" he had had to put his head in a sack and allow the younger generation to prod him with sticks had held the smoking room spellbound. At a place like Totleigh, where even on normal days human life was not safe, still worse excesses were to be expected. The glimpse or two I had had of the local Dead End kids had told me how tough a bunch they were and how sedulously they should be avoided by the man who knew what was good for him.

"I shall nip over to Brinkley in the car and have lunch with Uncle Tom. You at my side, I hope?"

"Impossible, I fear, sir. I have promised to assist Mr. Butterfield in the tea tent."

"Then you can tell me all about it."

"Very good, sir."

"If you survive."

"Precisely, sir."

It was a nice easy drive to Brinkley, and I got there well in advance of the luncheon hour. Aunt Dahlia wasn't there, having, as foreshadowed, popped up to London for the day, and Uncle Tom and I sat down alone to a repast in Anatole's best vein. Over the Suprême de Foie Gras au Champagne and the Neige aux Perles des Alpes I placed him in possession of the facts relating to the black amber statuette thing, and his relief at learning that Pop Bassett hadn't got a thousand-quid objet d'art for a fiver was so profound and the things he said about Pop B so pleasing to the ear that by the time I started back my dark mood had become sensibly lightened and optimism had returned to its throne.

After all, I reminded myself, it wasn't as if Gussie was going to be indefinitely under Madeline's eye. In due season he would buzz back to London and there would be able to tuck into the beefs and muttons till his ribs squeaked, confident that not a word of his activities would reach her. The effect of this would be to refill him with sweetness and light, causing him to write her loving letters which would carry him along till she emerged from this vegetarian phase and took up stamp collecting or something. I know the other sex and their sudden enthusiasms. They get these crazes and wallow in them for a while, but they soon become fed up and turn to other things. My Aunt Agatha once went in for politics, but it only took a few meetings at which she got the bird from hecklers to convince her that the cagey thing to do was to stay at home and attend to her fancy needlework, giving the whole enterprise a miss.

It was getting on for what is called the quiet evenfall when I dropped anchor at Totleigh Towers. I did my usual sneak to my room, and I had been there a few minutes when Jeeves came in.

"I saw you arrive, sir," he said, "and I thought you might be in need of refreshment."

I assured him that his intuition had not led him astray, and he said he would bring me a whiskey-and-s. immediately.

"I trust you found Mr. Travers in good health, sir."

I was able to reassure him there.

"He was a bit low when I blew in, but on receipt of my news about the whatnot blossomed like a flower. It would have done you good to have heard what he had to say about Pop Bassett. And talking of Pop Bassett, how did the school treat go off?"

"I think the juvenile element enjoyed the festivities, sir."

"How about you?"

"Sir?"

"You were all right? They didn't put your head in a sack and prod you with sticks?"

"No, sir. My share in the afternoon's events was confined to assisting in the tea tent."

"You speak lightly, Jeeves, but I've known some dark work to take place in school treat tea tents."

"It is odd that you should say that, sir, for it was while partaking of tea that a lad threw a hard-boiled egg at Sir Watkyn."

"And hit him?"

"On the left cheekbone, sir. It was most unfortunate."

I could not subscribe to this.

"I don't know why you say 'unfortunate.' Best thing that could have happened, in my opinion. The very first time I set eyes on Pop Bassett, in the picturesque environment of Bosher Street Police Court, I remember saying to myself that there sat a man to whom it would do all the good in the world to have hard-boiled eggs thrown at him. One of my crowd on that occasion, a lady accused of being drunk and disorderly and resisting the police, did, on receipt of

[121]

her sentence, throw her boot at him, but with a poor aim, succeeding only in beaning the magistrate's clerk. What's the boy's name?"

"I could not say, sir. His actions were cloaked in anonymity."

"A pity. I would have liked to reward him by sending camels bearing apes, ivory, and peacocks to his address. Did you see anything of Gussie in the course of the afternoon?"

"Yes, sir. Mr. Fink-Nottle, at Miss Bassett's insistence, played a large part in the proceedings and was, I am sorry to say, somewhat roughly handled by the younger revelers. Among other vicissitudes that he underwent, a child entangled its all-day sucker in his hair."

"That must have annoyed him. He's fussy about his hair."

"Yes, sir, he was visibly incensed. He detached the sweetmeat and threw it from him with a good deal of force, and by ill luck it struck Miss Byng's dog on the nose. Affronted by what he presumably mistook for an unprovoked assault, the animal bit Mr. Fink-Nottle in the leg."

"Poor old Gussie!"

"Yes, sir."

"Still, into each life some rain must fall."

"Precisely, sir. I will go and bring your whiskey-and-soda."

He had scarcely gone when Gussie blew in, limping a little but otherwise showing no signs of what Jeeves had called the vicissitudes he had undergone. He seemed, indeed, above rather than below his usual form, and I remember the phrase "the bulldog breed" passed through my mind. If Gussie was a sample of young England's stamina and fortitude, it seemed to me that the country's future was secure. It is not every nation that can produce sons capable of grinning, as he was doing, so shortly after being bitten by Aberdeen terriers.

"Oh, there you are, Bertie," he said. "Jeeves told me you were back. I looked in to borrow some cigarettes."

"Go ahead."

"Thanks," he said, filling his case. "I'm taking Emerald Stoker for a walk."

"You're *what?*"

"Or a row on the river. Whichever she prefers."

"But, Gussie—"

"Oh, before I forget. Pinker is looking for you. He says he wants to see you about something important."

"Never mind about Stinker. You can't take Emerald Stoker for walks."

"Can't I? Watch me."

"But—"

"Sorry, no time to talk now. I don't want to keep her waiting. So long; I must be off."

He left me plunged in thought, and not agreeable thought either. I think I have made it clear to the meanest i. that my whole future depended on Augustus Fink-Nottle sticking to the straight and narrow path and not blotting his copybook, and I could not but feel that by taking Emerald Stoker for walks he was skidding off the straight and narrow path and blotting his c. in no uncertain manner. That, at least, was, I was pretty sure, how an idealistic beazel like Madeline Bassett, already rendered hot under the collar by his subversive views on sunsets and Blessed Damozels, would regard it. It is not too much to say that when Jeeves returned with the whiskey-and-s., he found me all of a twitter and shaking on my stem.

I would have liked to put him abreast of this latest development, but, as I say, there are things we don't discuss, so

I merely drank deep of the flowing bowl and told him that Gussie had just been a pleasant visitor.

"He tells me Stinker Pinker wants to see me about something."

"No doubt with reference to the episode of Sir Watkyn and the hard-boiled egg, sir."

"Don't tell me it was Stinker who threw it."

"No, sir, the miscreant is believed to have been a lad in his early teens. But the young fellow's impulsive action has led to unfortunate consequences. It has caused Sir Watkyn to entertain doubts as to the wisdom of entrusting a vicarage to a curate incapable of maintaining order at a school treat. Miss Byng, while confiding this information to me, appeared greatly distressed. She had supposed—I quote her verbatim—that the thing was in the bag, and she is naturally much disturbed."

I drained my glass and lit a moody gasper. If Totleigh Towers wanted to turn me into a cynic, it was going the right way about it.

"There's a curse on this house, Jeeves. Broken blossoms and shattered hopes wherever you look. It seems to be something in the air. The sooner we're out of here, the better. I wonder if we couldn't—"

I had been about to add "make our getaway tonight," but at this moment the door flew open and Spode came bounding in, wiping the words from my lips and causing me to raise an eyebrow or two. I resented this habit he was developing of popping up out of a trap at me every other minute like a Demon King in pantomime, and only the fact that I couldn't think of anything restrained me from saying something pretty stinging. As it was, I wore the mask and spoke with the suavity of the perfect host.

"Ah, Spode. Come on in and take a few chairs," I said,

and was on the point of telling him that we Woosters kept
open house, when he interrupted me with the uncouth
abruptness so characteristic of these human gorillas. Roderick Spode may have had his merits, though I had never
been able to spot them, but his warmest admirer couldn't
have called him couth.

CHAPTER
FOURTEEN

"Have you seen Fink-Nottle?" he said.

I didn't like the way he spoke or the way he was looking. The lips, I noted, were twitching, and the eyes glittered with what I believe is called a baleful light. It seemed pretty plain to me that it was in no friendly spirit that he was seeking Gussie, so I watered down the truth a bit, as the prudent man does on these occasions.

"I'm sorry, no. I've only just got back from my uncle's place over Worcestershire way. Some urgent family business came up and I had to go and attend to it, so unfortunately missed the school treat. A great disappointment. You haven't seen Gussie, have you, Jeeves?"

He made no reply, possibly because he wasn't there. He generally slides discreetly off when the young master is entertaining the quality, and you never see him go. He just evaporates.

"Was it something important you wanted to see him about?"

"I want to break his neck."

My eyebrows, which had returned to normal, rose again. I also, if I remember rightly, pursed my lips.

"Well, really, Spode! Is this not becoming a bit thick? It's not so long ago that you were turning over in your mind the idea of breaking mine. I think you should watch yourself in this matter of neck-breaking and check the urge before it gets too strong a grip on you. No doubt you say to yourself that you can take it or leave it alone, but isn't there the danger of the thing becoming habit-forming? Why do you want to break Gussie's neck?"

He ground his teeth—at least that's what I think he did to them—and was silent for a space. Then, though there wasn't anyone within earshot but me, he lowered his voice.

"I can speak frankly to you, Wooster, because you, too, love her."

"Eh? Who?" I said. It should have been "whom," I suppose, but that didn't occur to me at the time.

"Madeline, of course."

"Oh, Madeline?"

"As I told you, I have always loved her, and her happiness is very dear to me. It is everything to me. To give her a moment's pleasure, I would cut myself in pieces."

I couldn't follow him there, but before I could go into the question of whether girls enjoy seeing people cut themselves in pieces he had resumed.

"It was a great shock to me when she became engaged to this man Fink-Nottle, but I accepted the situation because I

[127]

thought that that was where her happiness lay. Though stunned, I kept silent."

"Very white."

"I said nothing that would give her a suspicion of how I felt."

"Very pukka."

"It was enough for me that she should be happy. Nothing else mattered. But when Fink-Nottle turns out to be a libertine—"

"Who—Gussie?" I said, surprised. "The last chap I'd have attached such a label to. Pure as the driven s., I'd have thought, if not purer. What makes you think Gussie's a libertine?"

"The fact that less than ten minutes ago I saw him kissing the cook," said Spode through the teeth which I'm pretty sure he was grinding, and he dived out of the door and was gone.

How long I remained motionless, like a ventriloquist's dummy whose ventriloquist has gone off to the local and left it sitting, I cannot say. Probably not so very long, for when life returned to the rigid limbs and I legged it for open spaces to try to find Gussie and warn him of this V-shaped depression which was coming his way, Spode was still in sight. He was disappearing in a nor'-nor'easterly direction, so, not wanting to hobnob with him again while he was in this what you might call difficult mood, I pushed off sou'-sou'west and found that I couldn't have set my course more shrewdly. There was a sort of yew alley or rhododendron walk or some such thing confronting me, and as I entered it I saw Gussie. He was standing in a kind of trance, and his fatheadedness in standing when he ought to have been running like a rabbit smote me like a blow and lent an extra emphasis to the "Hoy!" with which I accosted him.

He turned, and as I approached him I noted that he seemed even more braced than when last seen. The eyes behind the horn-rimmed spectacles gleamed with a brighter light, and a smile wreathed his lips. He looked like a fish that's just learned that its rich uncle in Australia has pegged out and left it a packet.

"Ah, Bertie," he said, "we decided to go for a walk, not a row. We thought it might be a little chilly on the water. What a beautiful evening, Bertie, is it not?"

I couldn't see eye to eye with him there.

"It strikes you as that, does it? It doesn't me."

He seemed surprised.

"In what respect do you find it not up to sample?"

"I'll tell you in what respect I find it not up to sample. What's all this I hear about you and Emerald Stoker? Did you kiss her?"

The Soul's Awakening expression on his face became intensified. Before my revolted eyes, Augustus Fink-Nottle definitely smirked.

"Yes, Bertie, I did, and I'll do it again if it's the last thing I do. What a girl, Bertie! So kind, so sympathetic. She's my idea of a thoroughly womanly woman, and you don't see many of them around these days. I hadn't time when I was in your room to tell you about what happened at the school treat."

"Jeeves told me. He said Bartholomew bit you."

"And how right he was. The bounder bit me to the bone. And do you know what Emerald Stoker did? Not only did she coo over me like a mother comforting a favorite child, but she bathed and bandaged my lacerated leg. She was a ministering angel, the nearest thing to Florence Nightingale you could hope to find. It was shortly after she had done the swabbing and bandaging that I kissed her."

"Well, you shouldn't have kissed her."

Again he showed surprise. He had thought it, he said, a pretty sound idea.

"But you're engaged to Madeline."

I had hoped with these words to start his conscience working on all twelve cylinders, but something seemed to have gone wrong with the machinery, for he remained as calm and unmoved as the fish on ice he so closely resembled.

"Ah, Madeline," he said, "I was about to touch on Madeline. Shall I tell you what's wrong with Madeline Bassett? No heart. That's where she slips up. Lovely to look at, but nothing *here*," he said, tapping the left side of his chest. "Do you know how she reacted to that serious flesh wound of mine? She espoused Bartholomew's cause. She said the whole thing was my fault. She accused me of having teased the little blister. In short, she behaved like a louse. How different from Emerald Stoker. Do you know what Emerald Stoker did?"

"You told me."

"I mean in addition to binding up my wounds. She went straight off to the kitchen and cut me a package of sandwiches. I have them here," said Gussie, exhibiting a large parcel and eyeing it reverently. "Ham," he added in a voice that throbbed with emotion. "She made them for me with her own hands, and I think it was her thoughtfulness even more than her divine sympathy that showed me that she was the only girl in the world for me. The scales fell from my eyes, and I saw that what I had once felt for Madeline had been just a boyish infatuation. What I feel for Emerald Stoker is the real thing. In my opinion she stands alone, and I shall be glad if you will stop going about the place saying that she looks like a Pekingese."

[130]

"But, Gussie—"

He silenced me with an imperious wave of the ham sandwiches.

"It's no good your saying 'But, Gussie.' The trouble with you, Bertie, is that you haven't got it in you to understand true love. You're a mere butterfly flitting from flower to flower and sipping, like Freddie Widgeon and the rest of the half-wits of whom the Drones Club is far too full. A girl to you is just the plaything of an idle hour, and anything in the nature of a grand passion is beyond you. I'm different. I have depth. I'm a marrying man."

"But you can't marry Emerald Stoker."

"Why not? We're twin souls."

I thought for a moment of giving him a word portrait of old Stoker, to show him the sort of father-in-law he would be getting if he carried through the project he had in mind, but I let it go. Reason told me that a fellow who for months had been expecting to draw Pop Bassett as a father-in-law was not going to be swayed by an argument like that. However frank my description of him, Stoker could scarcely seem anything but a change for the better.

I stood there at a loss, and was still standing there at a loss, when I heard my name called and, looking behind me, saw Stinker and Stiffy. They were waving hands and things, and I gathered that they had come to thresh out with me the matter of Sir Watkyn Bassett and the hard-boiled egg.

The last thing I would have wished at this crucial point in my affairs was an interruption, for all my faculties should have been concentrated on reasoning with Gussie and trying to make him see the light, but it has often been said of Bertram Wooster that when a buddy in distress is drawn to his attention he forgets self. No matter what his commitments elsewhere, the distressed buddy has only to beckon and he is with him. With a brief word to Gussie that I would be back at an early date to resume our discussion, I hurried to where Stiffy and Stinker stood.

"Talk quick," I said. "I'm in conference. Too long to tell you all about it, but a serious situation has arisen. As, according to Jeeves, one has with you. From what he told me, I gathered that the odds against Stinker clicking as regards that vicarage have lengthened. More letting-I-dare-not-wait-upon-I-would-ness on Pop Bassett's part, he gave me to understand. Too bad."

"Of course, one can see it from Sir Watkyn's point of view," said Stinker, who, if he has a fault besides bumping into furniture and upsetting it, is always far too tolerant in his attitude toward the dregs of humanity. "He thinks that if I'd drilled the distinction between right and wrong more vigorously into the minds of the Infants Bible Class, the thing wouldn't have happened."

"I don't see why not," said Stiffy.

Nor did I. In my opinion, no amount of Sunday afternoon instruction would have been sufficient to teach a growing boy not to throw hard-boiled eggs at Sir Watkyn Bassett.

"But there's nothing I can do about it, is there?" I said.

"You bet there is," said Stiffy. "We haven't lost all hope of sweetening him. The great thing is to let his nervous system gradually recover its poise, and what we came to see you about, Bertie, was to tell you on no account to go near him till he's had a chance to simmer down. Don't seek him out. Leave him alone. The sight of you does something to him."

"No more than the sight of him does to me," I riposted warmly. I resented the suggestion that I had nothing better to do with my time than fraternize with ex-magistrates. "Certainly I'll avoid his society. It'll be a pleasure. Is that all?"

"That's all."

"Then I'll be getting back to Gussie," I said, and was starting to move off, when Stiffy uttered a sharp squeak.

"Gussie! That reminds me. There's something I wanted to tell him, something of vital concern to him, and I can't think how it slipped my mind. Gussie," she called, and Gussie, seeming to wake abruptly from a daydream, blinked and came over. "What are you doing hanging about here, Gussie?"

"Who, me? I was discussing something with Bertie, and he said he'd be back, when at liberty, to go into it further."

"Well, let me tell you that you've no time for discussing things with Bertie."

"Eh?"

"Or for saying 'Eh?' I met Roderick just now, and he asked me if I knew where you were, because he wants to tear you limb from limb, owing to his having seen you kiss the cook."

Gussie's jaw fell with a dull thud.

"You never told me that," he said to me, and one spotted the note of reproach in his voice.

"No, sorry, I forgot to mention it. But it's true. You'd better start coping. Run like a hare, is my advice."

He took it. Standing not on the order of his going, as the fellow said, he dashed off as if shot from a gun and was making excellent time when he was brought up short by colliding with Spode, who had at that moment entered left center.

CHAPTER
FIFTEEN

IT'S ALWAYS disconcerting to have even as small a chap as Gussie take you squarely in the midriff, as I myself can testify, having had the same experience down in Washington Square during a visit to New York. Washington Square is bountifully supplied with sad-eyed Italian kids who whiz to and fro on roller skates, and one of them, proceeding on his way with lowered head, rammed me in the neighborhood of the third waistcoat button at a high rate of m.p.h. It gave me a strange where-am-I feeling, and I imagine Spode's sensations were somewhat similar. His breath escaped him in a sharp "Oof!" and he swayed like some forest tree beneath the woodman's ax. But unfortunately Gussie had paused to sway, too, and this gave Spode time to steady himself on even keel and regroup his forces. Reaching out a hamlike hand, he attached it to the scruff of Gussie's neck and said, "Ha!"

"Ha!" is one of those things it's never easy to find the right reply to—it resembles "You!" in that respect—but Gussie was saved the necessity of searching for words by the fact that he was being shaken like a cocktail in a manner that precluded speech, if precluded is the word I want. His spectacles fell off and came to rest near where I was standing. I picked them up with a view to returning them to him when he had need of them, which I could see would not be immediately.

As this Fink-Nottle was a boyhood friend, with whom, as I have said, I had frequently shared my last bar of milk chocolate, and as it was plain that if someone didn't intervene pretty soon he was in danger of having all his internal organs shaken into a sort of macédoine or hash, the thought of taking some steps to put an end to this distressing scene naturally crossed my mind. The problem presenting several points of interest was, of course, what steps to take. My tonnage was quite insufficient to enable me to engage Spode in hand-to-hand conflict, and I toyed with the idea of striking him on the back of the head with a log of wood. But this project was rendered null and void by the fact that there were no logs of wood present. These yew alleys or rhododendron walks provide twigs and fallen leaves but nothing in the shape of logs capable of being used as clubs. And I had just decided that something might be accomplished by leaping on Spode's back and twining my arms around his neck when I heard Stiffy cry, "Harold!"

One gathered what she was driving at. Gussie was no particular buddy of hers, but she was a tenderhearted young prune and one always likes to save a fellow creature's life, if possible. She was calling on Stinker to get into the act and save Gussie's. And a quick look at him showed me that he was at a loss to know how to proceed. He stood there passing a finger thoughtfully over his chin, like a cat in an adage.

I knew what was stopping him getting action. It was not . . . it's on the tip of my tongue . . . begins with a p . . . I've heard Jeeves use the word . . . pusillanimity, that's it, meaning broadly that a fellow is suffering from a pronounced case of cold feet . . . it was not, as I was saying when I interrupted myself, pusillanimity that held him back. Under normal conditions lions could have taken his correspondence course, and had he encountered Spode on the football field, he would have had no hesitation in springing at his neck and twisting it into a lover's knot. The trouble was that he was a curate, and the brass hats of the Church look askance at curates who swat parishioners. Sock your flock, and you're sunk. So now he shrank from intervening, and when he did intervene, it was merely with the soft word that's supposed to turn away wrath.

"I say, you know, what?" he said.

I could have told him he was approaching the thing from the wrong angle. When a gorilla like Spode is letting his angry passions rise, there is little or no percentage in the mild remonstrance. Seeming to realize this, he advanced to where the blighter was now, or so it appeared, trying to strangle Gussie and laid a hand on his shoulder. Then, seeing that this, too, achieved no solid results, he pulled. There was a rending sound, and the clutching hand relaxed its grip.

I don't know if you've ever tried detaching a snow leopard of the Himalayas from its prey—probably not, as most people don't find themselves out that way much—but if you did, you would feel fairly safe in budgeting for a show of annoyance on the animal's part. It was the same with Spode. Incensed at what I suppose seemed to him this unwarrant-

[136]

able interference with his aims and objects, he hit Stinker on the nose, and all the doubts that had been bothering that man of God vanished in a flash.

I should imagine that if there's one thing that makes a fellow forget that he's in holy orders, it's a crisp punch on the beezer. A moment before, Stinker had been all concern about the disapproval of his superiors in the cloth, but now, as I read his mind, he was saying to himself, "To hell with my superiors in the cloth," or however a curate would put it; "let them eat cake."

It was a superb spectacle while it lasted, and I was able to understand what people meant when they spoke of the Church Militant. A good deal to my regret, it did not last long. Spode was full of the will to win, but Stinker had the science. It was not for nothing that he had added a boxing blue to his football blue when at the old Alma Mater. There was a brief mix-up, and the next thing one observed was Spode on the ground, looking like the corpse which had been in the water several days. His left eye was swelling visibly, and a referee could have counted a hundred over him without eliciting a response.

Stiffy, with a brief "At-a-boy," led Stinker off, no doubt to bathe his nose and stanch the vital flow, which was considerable, and I handed Gussie his glasses. He stood twiddling them in a sort of trance, and I made a suggestion which I felt was in his best interests.

"Not to presume to dictate, Gussie, but wouldn't it be wise to remove yourself before Spode comes to? From what I know of him, I think he's one of those fellows who wake up cross."

I have seldom seen anyone move quicker. We were out of the yew alley, if it was a yew alley, or the rhododendron walk, if that's what it was, almost before the words had left my lips. We continued to set a good pace, but eventually we slowed up a bit and he was able to comment on the recent scene.

"That was a ghastly experience, Bertie," he said.

"Can't have been at all pleasant," I agreed.

"My whole past life seemed to flash before me."

"That's odd. You weren't drowning."

"No, but the principle's the same. I can tell you I was thankful when Pinker made his presence felt. What a splendid chap he is."

"One of the best."

"That's what today's Church needs—more curates capable of hauling off and letting fellows like Spode have it where it does most good. One feels so safe when he's around."

I put a point which seemed to have escaped his notice.

"But he won't always be around. He has Infants Bible Classes and Mothers Meetings and all that sort of thing to occupy his time. And don't forget that Spode, though crushed to earth, will rise again."

His jaw sagged a bit.

"I never thought of that."

"If you take my advice, you'll clear out and go underground for a while. Stiffy would lend you her car."

"I believe you're right," he said, adding something about out of the mouths of babes and sucklings, which I thought a bit offensive. "I'll leave this evening."

"Without saying goodbye."

"Of course without saying goodbye. No, don't go that way. Keep bearing to the left. I want to go to the kitchen garden. I told Em I'd meet her there."

"You told *who?*"

"Emerald Stoker. Who did you think I meant? She had

to go to the kitchen garden and gather beans and things for tonight's dinner."

And there, sure enough, she was with a large basin in her hands, busy about her domestic duties.

"Here's Bertie, Em," said Gussie, and she whisked round, spilling a bean or two.

I was disturbed to see how every freckle on her face lit up as she looked at him, as if she were gazing on some lovely sight, which was far from being the case. In me she didn't seem much interested. A brief "Hullo, Bertie" appeared to cover it as far as I was concerned, her whole attention being earmarked for Gussie. She was staring at him as a mother might have stared at a loved child who had shown up at the home after a clash with one of the neighborhood children. Until then I had been too agitated to notice how disheveled his encounter with Spode had left him, but I now saw that his general appearance was that of something that has been passed through a wringer.

"What . . . *what* have you been doing to yourself?" She ejaculated, if that's the word. "You look like a devastated area."

"Inevitable in the circs," I said. "He's been having a spot of unpleasantness with Spode."

"Is that the man you were telling me about? The human gorilla?"

"That's the one."

"What happened?"

"Spode tried to shake the stuffing out of him."

"You poor precious lambkin," said Emerald, addressing Gussie, not me. "Gosh, I wish I had him here for a minute. I'd teach him!"

And by what I have always thought an odd coincidence her wish was granted. A crashing sound like that made by a herd of hippopotami going through the reeds on a river-bank attracted my notice and I beheld Spode approaching at the rate of knots with the obvious intention of resuming at as early a date as possible his investigations into the color of Gussie's insides which Stinker's intervention had compelled him to file under the head of unfinished business. In predicting that this menace in the treatment, though crushed to earth, would rise again, I had been perfectly correct.

There seemed to me a strong resemblance in the newcomer's manner to that of those Assyrians who, so we learn from sources close to them, came down like a wolf on the fold with their cohorts all gleaming with purple and gold. He could have walked straight into their camp, and they would have laid down the red carpet for him, recognizing him instantly as one of the boys.

But where the Assyrians had had the bulge on him was that they weren't going to find in the fold a motherly young woman with strong wrists and a basin in her hands. This basin appeared to be constructed of some thickish form of china, and as Spode grabbed Gussie and started to go into the old shaking routine it descended on the back of his head with what some call a dull and others a sickening thud. It broke into several fragments, but by that time its mission had been accomplished. His powers of resistance sapped, no doubt, by his recent encounter with the Rev. H. P. Pinker, Spode fell to earth he knew not where and lay there looking peaceful. I remember thinking at the time that this was not his lucky day, and it just showed, I thought, that it's always a mistake to be a louse in human shape, as he had been from birth, because sooner or later retribution is bound to overtake you. As I recall Jeeves putting it once, the mills of God grind slowly, but they grind exceeding small, or words to that effect.

For a space Emerald Stoker stood surveying her handi-work with a satisfied smile on her face, and I didn't blame her for looking a bit smug, for she had unquestionably fought the good fight. Then suddenly, with a quick "Oh, golly," she was off like a nymph surprised while bathing, and a moment later I understood what had caused this mo-bility. She had seen Madeline Bassett approaching, and no cook likes to have to explain to her employer why she has been bonneting her employer's guests with china basins.

As Madeline's eyes fell on the remains, they widened to the size of golf balls and she looked at Gussie as if he had been a mass murderer she wasn't very fond of.

"What have you been doing to Roderick?" she demanded.

"Eh?" said Gussie.

"I said, What have you done to Roderick?"

Gussie adjusted his spectacles and shrugged a shoulder.

"Oh, that? I merely chastised him. The fellow had only himself to blame. He asked for it, and I had to teach him a lesson."

"You brute!"

"Not at all. He had the option of withdrawing. He must have foreseen what would happen when he saw me remove my glasses. When I remove my glasses, those who know what's good for them take to the hills."

"I hate you, I hate you!" cried Madeline, a thing I didn't know anyone ever said except in the second act of a musical comedy.

"You do?" said Gussie.

"Yes, I do. I loathe you."

"Then, in that case," said Gussie, "I shall now eat a ham sandwich."

And this he proceeded to do with a sort of wolfish gusto

[141]

that sent cold shivers down my spine, and Madeline shrieked sharply.

"This is the end!" she said, another thing you don't often hear.

When things between two once loving hearts have hotted up to this extent, it is always the prudent course for the innocent bystander to edge away, and this I did. I started back to the house, and in the drive I met Jeeves. He was at the wheel of Stiffy's car. Beside him, looking like a Scotch elder rebuking sin, was the dog Bartholomew.

"Good evening, sir," he said. "I have been taking this little fellow to the veterinary surgeon. Miss Byng was uneasy because he bit Mr. Fink-Nottle. She was afraid he might have caught something. I am glad to say the surgeon has given him a clean bill of health."

"Jeeves," I said. "I have a tale of horror to relate."

"Indeed, sir?"

"The lute is mute," I said, and as briefly as possible put him in possesion of the facts. When I had finished, he agreed that it was most disturbing.

"But I fear there is nothing to be done, sir."

I reeled. I have grown so accustomed to seeing Jeeves solve every problem, however sticky, that this frank confession of his inability to deliver the goods unmanned me.

"You're baffled?"

"Yes, sir."

"At a loss?"

"Precisely, sir. Possibly at some future date a means of adjusting matters will occur to me, but at the moment, I regret to say, I can think of nothing. I am sorry, sir."

I shrugged the shoulders. The iron had entered into my soul, but the upper lip was stiff.

"It's all right, Jeeves. Not your fault if a thing like this lays you a stymie. Drive on, Jeeves," I said, and he drove on. The dog Bartholomew gave me an unpleasantly superior look as they moved off, as if asking me if I were saved.

I pushed along to my room, the only spot in this joint of terror where anything in the nature of peace and quiet was to be had, not that even there one got much of it. The fierce rush of life at Totleigh Towers had got me down, and I wanted to be alone.

I suppose I must have sat there for more than half an hour, trying to think what was to be done for the best, and then, out of what I have heard Jeeves describe as the welter of emotions, one coherent thought emerged, and that was that if I didn't shortly get a snifter, I would expire in my tracks. It was now the cocktail hour, and I knew that, whatever his faults, Sir Watkyn Bassett provided apéritifs for his guests. True, I had promised Stiffy that I would avoid his society, but I had not anticipated then that this emergency would arise. It was a straight choice between betraying her trust and perishing where I sat, and I decided on the former alternative.

I found Pop Bassett in the drawing room with a well-laden tray at his elbow and hurried forward, licking my lips. To say that he looked glad to see me would be overstating it, but he offered me a life saver and I accepted it gratefully. An awkward silence of about twenty minutes followed, and then, just as I had finished my second and was fishing for the olive, Stiffy entered. She gave me a quick reproachful look, and I could see that her trust in Bertram's promises would never be the same again, but it was to Pop Bassett that she directed her attention.

"Hullo, Uncle Watkyn."

"Good evening, my dear."

"Having a spot before dinner?"

"I am."

"You think you are," said Stiffy, "but you aren't, and I'll tell you why. There isn't going to be any dinner. The cook's eloped with Gussie Fink-Nottle."

CHAPTER
SIXTEEN

I WONDER if you have ever noticed a rather peculiar thing—viz., how differently the same news item can affect two different people? I mean, you tell something to Jones and Brown, let us say, and while Jones sits plunged in gloom and looking licked to a splinter, Brown gives three rousing cheers and goes into a buck-and-wing dance. And the same thing is true of Smith and Robinson. Often struck me as curious, that has.

It was so now. Listening to the recent heated exchanges between Madeline Bassett and Gussie hadn't left me what you might call optimistic, but the heart bowed down with weight of woe to weakest hope will cling, as the fellow said, and I had tried to tell myself that their mutual love, though admittedly having taken it on the chin at the moment, might eventually get cracking again, causing all to be forgotten and forgiven. I mean to say, remorse has frequently been known to set in after a dustup between a couple of troth plighters, with all that Sorry-I-was-cross and Can-you-ever-forgive-me stuff, and love, after being down in the cellar for a time with no takers, perks up and carries on again as good as new. Oh, blessings on the falling out that all the more endears is the way I heard Jeeves put it once.

But at Stiffy's words this hope collapsed as if it had been struck on the back of the head with a china basin containing beans, and I sank forward in my chair, the face buried in the hands. It is always my policy to look on the bright side, but in order to do this you have to have a bright side to look on, and under existing conditions there wasn't one. This, as Madeline Bassett would have said, was the end. I had come to this house as a *raisonneur* to bring the young folks together, but however much of a *raisonneur* you are, you can't bring young folks together if one of them elopes with somebody else. You are not merely hampered but shackled. So now, as I say, I sank forward in my chair, the f. buried in the h.

To Pop Bassett, on the other hand, this bit of front-page news had plainly come as rare and refreshing fruit. My face being buried as stated, I couldn't see if he went into a buck-and-wing dance, but I should think it highly probable that he did a step or two, for when he spoke you could tell from the timbre of his voice that he was feeling about as pepped up as a man can feel without bursting.

One could understand his fizziness, of course. Of all the prospective sons-in-law in existence, Gussie, with the possible exception of Bertram Wooster, was the one he would have chosen last. He had viewed him with concern from the start, and if he had been living back in the days when fathers called the shots in the matter of their daughters' marriages, would have forbidden the banns without a second thought.

Gussie once told me that when he, Gussie, was introduced to him, Bassett, as the fellow who was to marry his, Bassett's, offspring, he, Bassett, had stared at him with his jaw dropping and then in a sort of strangled voice had said, *"What!"* Incredulously, if you see what I mean, as if he were hoping that they were just playing a jolly practical joke on him and that in due course the real chap would jump out from behind a chair and say, "April fool!" And when he, Bassett, at last got on to it that there was no deception and that Gussie was really what he had drawn, he went off into a corner and sat there motionless, refusing to speak when spoken to.

Little wonder, then, that Stiffy's announcement had bucked him up like a dose of Doctor Somebody's Tonic Swamp Juice, which acts directly on the red corpuscles and imparts a gentle glow.

"Eloped?" he gurgled.

"That's right."

"With the cook?"

"With none other. That's why I said there wasn't going to be any dinner. We shall have to make do with hard-boiled eggs, if there are any left over from the treat."

The mention of hard-boiled eggs made Pop Bassett wince for a moment, and one could see that his thoughts had flitted back to the tea tent, but he was far too happy to allow sad memories to trouble him for long. With a wave of the hand he dismissed dinner as something that didn't matter one way or the other. The Bassetts, the wave suggested, could rough it if they had to.

"Are you sure of your facts, my dear?"

"I met them as they were starting off. Gussie said he hoped I wouldn't mind him borrowing my car."

"You reassured him, I trust?"

"Oh, yes. I said, 'That's all right, Gussie. Help yourself.' "

"Good girl. Good girl. An excellent response. Then they have really gone?"

"With the wind."

"And they plan to get married?"

"As soon as Gussie can get a special license. You have to apply to the Archbishop of Canterbury, and I'm told he stings you for quite a bit. "

"Money well spent."

"That's how Gussie feels. He told me he was dropping the cook at Bertie's aunt's place and then going on to London to confer with the Archbish. He's full of zeal."

This extraordinary statement that Gussie was landing Emerald Stoker on Aunt Dahlia brought my head up with a jerk. I found myself speculating on how the old flesh and blood was going to take the intrusion, and it gave me rather an awed feeling to think how deep Gussie's love for his Em must be, to make him face such fearful risks. The aged relative has a strong personality and finds no difficulty, when displeased, in reducing the object of her displeasure to a spot of grease in a matter of minutes. I am told that sportsmen whom in her hunting days she had occasion to rebuke for riding over hounds were never the same again and for months would go about in a sort of stupor, starting at sudden noises.

My head being now up, I was able to see Pop Bassett, and I found that he was regarding me with an eye so benevolent that I could hardly believe that this was the same ex-magistrate with whom I had so recently been hobnobbing, if you can call it hobnobbing when a couple of fellows sit in a couple of chairs for twenty minutes without saying a word to each other. It was plain that joy had made him the friend of all the world, even to the extent of allowing him to look at Bertram without a shudder. He was more like something out of Dickens than anything human.

"Your glass is empty, Mr. Wooster," he cried buoyantly. "May I refill it?"

I said he might. I had had two, which is generally my limit, but with my aplomb shattered as it was I felt that a third wouldn't hurt. Indeed, I would have been willing to go even more deeply into the thing. I once read about a man who used to drink twenty-six martinis before dinner, and the conviction was beginning to steal over me that he had had the right idea.

"Roderick tells me," he proceeded, as sunny as if a crack of his had been greeted with laughter in court, "that the reason you were unable to be with us at the school treat this afternoon was that urgent family business called you to Brinkley Court. I trust everything turned out satisfactorily?"

"Oh yes, thanks."

"We all missed you, but business before pleasure, of course. How was your uncle? You found him well, I hope?"

"Yes, he was fine."

"And your aunt?"

"She had gone to London."

"Indeed? You must have been sorry not to have seen her. I know few women I admire more. So hospitable. So breezy. I have seldom enjoyed anything more than my recent visit to her house."

I think his exuberance would have led him to continue in the same strain indefinitely, but at this point Stiffy came out of the thoughtful silence into which she had fallen. She had been standing there regarding him with a speculative eye, as if debating within herself whether or not to start some-

[149]

thing, and now she gave the impression that her mind was made up.

"I'm glad to see you so cheerful, Uncle Watkyn. I was afraid my news might have upset you."

"Upset me!" said Pop Bassett incredulously. "Whatever put that idea in your head?"

"Well, you're short one son-in-law."

"It is precisely that that has made this the happiest day of my life."

"Then you can make it the happiest of mine," said Stiffy, striking while the iron was h. "By giving Harold that vicarage."

Most of my attention, as you may well imagine, being concentrated on contemplating the soup in which I was immersed, I cannot say whether or not Pop Bassett hesitated, but if he did, it was only for an instant. No doubt for a second or two the vision of that hard-boiled egg rose before him and he was conscious again of the resentment he had been feeling at Stinker's failure to keep a firm hand on the junior members of his flock, but the thought that Augustus Fink-Nottle was not to be his son-in-law drove the young cleric's shortcomings from his mind. Filled with the milk of human kindness so nearly to the brim that you could almost hear it sloshing about inside him, he was in no shape to deny anyone anything. I really believe that if at this point in the proceedings I had tried to touch him for a fiver, he would have parted without a cry.

"Of course, of course, of course, of course," he said, caroling like one of Jeeves' larks on the wing. "I am sure that Pinker will make an excellent vicar."

"The best," said Stiffy. "He's wasted as a curate. No scope. Running under wraps. Unleash him as a vicar, and he'll be the talk of the established church. He's as hot as a pistol."

"I have always had the highest opinion of Harold Pinker."

"I'm not surprised. All the nibs feel the same. They know he's got what it takes. Very sound on doctrine and can preach like a streak."

"Yes, I enjoy his sermons. Manly and straightforward."

"That's because he's one of these healthy outdoor open-air men. Muscular Christianity, that's his dish. He used to play football for England."

"Indeed?"

"He was what's called a prop forward."

"Really?"

At the words "prop forward" I had, of course, started visibly. I hadn't known that that's what Stinker was, and I was thinking how ironical life could be. I mean to say, there was Plank searching high and low for a forward of this nature, saying to himself that he would pretty soon have to give up the hopeless quest, and here was I in a position to fill the bill for him but, owing to the strained condition of our relations, unable to put him on to this good thing. Very sad, I felt, and the thought occurred to me, as it had often done before, that one ought to be kind even to the very humblest, because you never know when they may not come in useful.

"Then may I tell Harold that the balloon's going up?" said Stiffy.

"I beg your pardon?"

"I mean it's official about this vicarage?"

"Certainly, certainly, certainly."

"Oh, Uncle Watkyn! How can I thank you?"

"Quite all right, my dear," said Pop Bassett, more Dickensy than ever. "And now," he went on, parting from his moorings and making for the door, "you will excuse me, Stephanie, and you, Mr. Wooster. I must go to Madeline and—"

"Congratulate her?"

"I was about to say dry her tears."

"If any."

"You think she will not be in a state of dejection?"

"Would any girl be, who's been saved by a miracle from having to marry Gussie Fink-Nottle?"

"True. Very true," said Pop Bassett, and he was out of the room like one of those wing three-quarters who, even if they can't learn to give the reverse pass, are fast.

If there had been any uncertainty as to whether Sir Watkyn Bassett had done a buck-and-wing dance, there was none about Stiffy doing one now. She pirouetted freely, and the dullest eye could discern that it was only the fact that she hadn't one on that kept her from strewing roses from her hat. I had seldom seen a young shrimp so above herself. And I, having Stinker's best interests at heart, packed all my troubles in the old kit bag for the time being and rejoiced with her. If there's one thing Bertram Wooster is and always has been nippy at, it's forgetting his personal worries when a pal is celebrating some stroke of good fortune.

For some time Stiffy monopolized the conversation, not letting me get a word in edgeways. Women are singularly gifted in this respect. The frailest of them has the lung power of a gramophone record and the flow of speech of a Regimental Sergeant Major. I have known my Aunt Agatha to go on calling me names long after you would have supposed that both breath and inventiveness would have given out.

Her theme was the stupendous bit of good luck which was about to befall Stinker's new parishioners, for they would be getting not only the perfect vicar, a saintly character who would do the square thing by their souls, but in addition the sort of vicar's wife you dream about. It was only when she paused after drawing a picture of herself doling out soup to the deserving poor and asking in a gentle voice after their rheumatism that I was able to rise to a point of order. In the midst of all the joyfulness and backslapping a sobering thought had occurred to me.

"I agree with you," I said, "that this would appear to be the happy ending, and I can quite see how you have arrived at the conclusion that it's the maddest, merriest day of all the glad new year, but there's something you ought to give a thought to, and it seems to me you're overlooking it."

"What's that? I didn't think I'd missed anything."

"This promise of Pop Bassett's to give you the vicarage."

"All in order, surely? What's your kick?"

"I was only thinking that, if I were you, I'd get it in writing."

This stopped her as if she had bumped into a prop forward. The ecstatic animation faded from her face, to be replaced by the anxious look and the quick chewing of the lower lip. It was plain that I had given her food for thought.

"You don't think Uncle Watkyn would double-cross us?"

"There are no limits to what your foul Uncle Watkyn can do, if the mood takes him," I responded gravely. "I wouldn't trust him an inch. Where's Stinker?"

"Out on the lawn, I think."

"Then get hold of him and bring him here and have Pop Bassett embody the thing in the form of a letter."

"I suppose you know you're making my flesh creep?"

"Merely pointing out the road to safety."

She mused awhile, and the lower lip got a bit more chewing done to it.

"All right," she said at length. "I'll fetch Harold."

"And it wouldn't hurt to bring a couple of lawyers, too," I said as she whizzed past me.

[153]

It was about five minutes later, as I was falling into a reverie and brooding once more on the extreme stickiness of my affairs, that Jeeves came in and told me I was wanted on the telephone.

CHAPTER
SEVENTEEN

I PALED beneath my tan.

"Who is it, Jeeves?"

"Mrs. Travers, sir."

Precisely what I had feared. It was, as I have indicated, an easy drive from Totleigh Towers to Brinkley Court, and in his exhilarated state Gussie would no doubt have kept a firm foot on the accelerator and given the machine all the gas at his disposal. I presumed that he and girl friend must have just arrived and that this telephone call was Aunt Dahlia what-the-helling. Knowing how keenly the old bean resented being made the recipient of anything in the nature of funny business, into which category Gussie's butting in uninvited with his Em in attendance would unquestionably fall, I braced myself for the coming storm with as much fortitude as I could muster.

You might say, of course, that his rash act was no fault of mine and had nothing to do with me, but it's practically routine for aunts to blame nephews for everything that happens. It seems to be what nephews are for. It was only by an oversight, I have always felt, that my Aunt Agatha omitted to hold me responsible a year or two ago when her son, young Thos, nearly got sacked from the scholastic institution which he attends for breaking out at night in order to go and shy for coconuts at the local amusement park.

"How did she seem, Jeeves?"

"Sir?"

"Did she give you the impression that she was splitting a gusset?"

"Not particularly, sir. Mrs. Travers' voice is always robust. Would there be any reason why she should be splitting the gusset to which you refer?"

"You bet there would. No time to tell you now, but the skies are darkening and the air is full of V-shaped depressions off the coast of Iceland."

"I am sorry, sir."

"Nor are you the only one. Who was the fellow—or fellows, for I believe there was more than one—who went into the burning fiery furnace?"

"Shadrach, Meshach, and Abednego, sir."

"That's right. The names were on the tip of my tongue. I read about them when I won my Scripture Knowledge prize at school. Well, I know just how they must have felt. Aunt Dahlia?" I said, for I had now reached the instrument.

I had been expecting to have my ear scorched with well-chosen words, but to my surprise she seemed in merry mood. There was no suggestion of recrimination in her voice.

"Hullo there, you young menace to western civilization," she boomed. "How are you? Still ticking over?"

"To a certain extent. And you?"

"I'm fine. Did I interrupt you in the middle of your tenth cocktail?"

"My third," I corrected. "I usually stay steady at two, but Pop Bassett insisted on replenishing my glass. He's a bit above himself at the moment and very much the master of the revels. I wouldn't put it past him to have an ox roasted whole in the marketplace, if he can find an ox."

"Stinko, is he?"

"Not perhaps stinko, but certainly effervescent."

"Well, if you can suspend your drunken orgy for a minute or two, I'll tell you the news from home. I got back from London a quarter of an hour ago, and what do you think I found waiting on the mat? That newt-collecting freak Spink-Bottle, accompanied by a girl who looks like a Pekingese with freckles."

I drew a deep breath and embarked on my speech for the defense. If Bertram was to be put in the right light, now was the moment. True, her manner so far had been affable and she had given no sign of being about to go off with a bang, but one couldn't be sure that that wasn't because she was just biding her time. It's never safe to dismiss aunts lightly at times like this.

"Yes," I said, "I heard he was on his way, complete with freckled human Pekingese. I am sorry, Aunt Dahlia, that you should have been subjected to this unwarrantable intrusion, and I would like to make it abundantly clear that it was not the outcome of any advice or encouragement from me. I was in total ignorance of his intentions. Had he confided in me his purpose of inflicting his presence on you, I should have—"

Here I paused, for she had asked me rather brusquely to put a sock in it.

"Stop babbling, you ghastly young gas bag. What's all this silver-tongued orator stuff about?"

"I was merely expressing my regret that you should have been subjected—"

"Well, don't. There's no need to apologize. I couldn't be more pleased. I admit that I'm always happier when I don't have Spink-Bottle breathing down the back of my neck and taking up space in the house which I require for other purposes, but the girl was as welcome as manna in the wilderness."

Having won that prize for Scripture Knowledge I was speaking of, I had no difficulty in grasping her allusion. She was referring to an incident which occurred when the children of Israel were crossing some desert or other and were sorely in need of refreshment, rations being on the slender side. And they were just saying to one another how well a spot of manna would go down and regretting that there was none in the quartermaster's stores when blowed if a whole wad of the stuff didn't descend from the skies, just making their day.

Her words had of course surprised me somewhat, and I asked her why Emerald Stoker had been as welcome as manna in the w.

"Because her arrival brought sunshine into a stricken home. There couldn't have been a smoother piece of timing. You didn't see Anatole when you were over here this afternoon, did you?"

"No. Why?"

"I was wondering if you had noticed anything wrong with him. Shortly after you left, he developed a *mal au foie* or whatever he called it and took to his bed."

"I'm sorry."

"So was Tom. He was looking forward gloomily to a

[158]

dinner cooked by the kitchen maid, who, though a girl of many sterling merits, always adopts the scorched-earth policy when preparing a meal, and you know what his digestion's like. Conditions looked dark, and then Spink-Bottle suddenly revealed that this Pekingese of his was an experienced chef, and she's taken over. Who is she? Do you know anything about her?"

I was, of course, able to supply the desired information.

"She's the daughter of a well-to-do American millionaire called Stoker, who, I imagine, will be full of strange oaths when he hears she's married Gussie, the latter being, as you will concede, not everybody's cup of tea."

"So he isn't going to marry Madeline Bassett?"

"No, the fixture has been scratched."

"That's definite, is it?"

"Yes."

"You can't have been much success as a *raisonneur*."

"No."

"Well, I think she'll make Spink-Bottle a good wife. Seems a very nice girl."

"Few better."

"But this leaves you in rather a spot, doesn't it? If Madeline Bassett is now at large, won't she expect you to fill in?"

"That, aged relative, is the fear that haunts me."

"Has Jeeves nothing to suggest?"

"He says he hasn't. But I've known him on previous occasions to be temporarily baffled and then suddenly to wave his magic wand and fix everything up. So I haven't entirely lost hope."

"No, I expect you'll wriggle out of it somehow, as you always do. I wish I had a fiver for every time you've been within a step of the altar rails and have managed to escape unscathed. I remember you telling me once that you had faith in your star."

"Quite. Still, it's no good trying to pretend that peril doesn't loom. It looms like the dickens. The corner in which I find myself is tight."

"And you would like to get that way, too, I suppose? All right, you can get back to your orgy when I've told you why I rang you up."

"Haven't you?" I said, surprised.

"Certainly not. You don't catch me wasting time and money chatting with you about your amours. Here is the nub. You know that black amber thing of Bassett's?"

"The statuette? Of course."

"I want to buy it for Tom. I've come into a bit of money. The reason I went to London today was to see my lawyer about a legacy someone's left me. Old school friend, if that's of any interest to you. It works out at about a couple of thousand quid, and I want you to get that statuette for me."

"It's going to be pretty hard to get away with it."

"Oh, you'll manage. Go as high as fifteen hundred pounds, if you have to. I suppose you couldn't just slip it in your pocket? It would save a lot of overhead. But probably that's asking too much of you, so tackle Bassett and get him to sell it."

"Well, I'll do my best. I know how much Uncle Tom covets that statuette. Rely on me, Aunt Dahlia."

"That's my boy."

I returned to the drawing room in somewhat pensive mood, for my relations with Pop Bassett were such that it was going to be embarrassing trying to do business with him, but I was relieved that the aged relative had dismissed the idea of purloining the thing. Surprised, too, as well as relieved, because the stern lesson association with her over the years has taught me is that when she wants to do a loved husband a good turn, she is seldom fussy about the methods employed at that end. It was she who had initiated, if that's the word I want, the theft of the cow creamer, and you would have thought she would have wanted to save money on the current deal. Her view has always been that if a collector pinches something from another collector, it doesn't count as stealing, and of course there may be something in it. Pop Bassett, when at Brinkley, would unquestionably have looted Uncle Tom's collection, had he not been closely watched. These collectors have about as much conscience as the smash-and-grab fellows for whom the police are always spreading dragnets.

I was musing along these lines and trying to think what would be the best way of approaching Pop, handicapped as I would be by the fact that he shuddered like a jelly in a high wind every time he saw me and preferred when in my presence to sit and stare before him without uttering, when the door opened and Spode came in.

CHAPTER
EIGHTEEN

THE FIRST THING that impressed itself on the senses was that
he had about as spectacular a black eye as you could meet
with in a month of Sundays, and I found myself at a momentary loss to decide how it was best to react to it. I mean,
some fellows with bunged-up eyes want sympathy, others
prefer that you pretend that you've noticed nothing unusual
in their appearance. I came to the conclusion that it was
wisest to greet him with a careless "Ah, Spode," and I did
so, though I suppose, looking back, that "Ah, Sidcup"
would have been more suitable; and it was as I spoke that
I became aware that he was glaring at me in a sinister
manner with the eye that wasn't closed. I have spoken of
these eyes of his as being capable of opening an oyster at
sixty paces, and even when only one of them was functioning

the impact of his gaze was disquieting. I have known my Aunt Agatha's gaze to affect me in the same way.

"I was looking for you, Wooster," he said.

He uttered the words in the unpleasant rasping voice which had once kept his followers on the jump. Before succeeding to his new title, he had been one of those Dictators who were fairly common at one time in the metropolis and had gone about with a mob of underlings wearing black shorts and shouting "Heil, Spode!" or words along those general lines. He gave it up when he became Lord Sidcup, but he was still apt to address all and sundry as if he were ticking off some erring member of his entourage whose shorts had got a patch on them.

"Oh, were you?" I said.

"I was." He paused for a moment, continuing to give me the eye; then he said, "So!"

"So!" is another of those things like "You!" and "Ha!" which it's never easy to find the right answer to. Nothing in the way of a comeback suggested itself to me, so I merely lit a cigarette in what I intended to be a nonchalant manner, though I may have missed it by a considerable margin, and he proceeded.

"So I was right!"

"Eh?"

"In my suspicions."

"Eh?"

"They have been confirmed."

"Eh?"

"Stop saying 'Eh?' you miserable worm, and listen to me."

I humored him. You might have supposed that having so recently seen him knocked base over apex by the Rev. H. P. Pinker and subsequently laid out cold by Emerald Stoker and her basin of beans I would have regarded him

[163]

with contempt as pretty small-time stuff and rebuked him sharply for calling me a miserable worm, but the idea never so much as crossed my mind. He had suffered reverses, true, but they had left him with his spirit unbroken and the muscles of his brawny arms just as much like iron bands as they had always been, and the way I looked at it was that if he wanted me to go easy on the word "Eh?" he had only to say so.

Continuing to pierce me with the eye that was still on duty, he said, "I happened to be passing through the hall just now."

"Oh?"

"I heard you talking on the telephone."

"Oh?"

"You were speaking to your aunt."

"Oh?"

"Don't keep saying 'Oh?' blast you."

Well, these restrictions were making it a bit hard for me to hold up my end of the conversation, but there seemed nothing to be done about it. I maintained a rather dignified silence, and he resumed his remarks.

"Your aunt was urging you to steal Sir Watkyn's amber statuette."

"She wasn't!"

"Pardon me. I thought you would try to deny the charge, so I took the precaution of jotting down your actual words. The statuette was mentioned and you said, 'It's going to be pretty hard to get away with it.' She then presumably urged you to spare no effort, for you said, 'Well, I'll do my best. I know how much Uncle Tom covets that statuette. Rely on me, Aunt Dahlia.' What the devil are you gargling about?"

"Not gargling," I corrected. "Laughing lightly. Because you've got the whole thing wrong, though I must say the

[164]

way you've managed to record the dialogue does you a good deal of credit. Do you use shorthand?"

"How do you mean I've got it wrong?"

"Aunt Dahlia was asking me to try to buy the thing from Sir Watkyn."

He snorted and said "Ha!" and I thought it a bit unjust that he should say "Ha!" if I wasn't allowed to say "Eh?" and "Oh?" There should always be a certain give-and-take in these matters, or where are you?

"Do you expect me to believe that?"

"Don't you believe it?"

"No, I don't. I'm not an ass."

This, of course, was a debatable point, as I once heard Jeeves describe it, but I didn't press it.

"I know that aunt of yours," he proceeded. "She would steal the filling of your back teeth if she thought she could do it without detection." He paused for a moment, and I knew that he was thinking of the cow creamer. He had always—and, I must admit, not without reason—suspected the old flesh and blood of being the motive force behind its disappearance, and I imagine it had been a nasty knock to him that nothing could be proved. "Well, I strongly advise you, Wooster, not to let her make a cat's-paw of you this time, because if you're caught, as you certainly will be, you'll be for it. Don't think that Sir Watkyn will hush the thing up to avoid a scandal. You'll go to prison, that's where you'll go. He dislikes you intensely, and nothing would please him more than to be able to give you a long stretch without the option."

I thought this showed a vindictive spirit in the old wart-hog, and one that I deplored, but I felt it would be injudicious to say so. I merely nodded understandingly. I was thankful that there was no danger of this contingency, as

Jeeves would have called it, arising. Strong in the knowledge that nothing would induce me to pinch their ruddy statuette, I was able to remain calm and nonchalant, or as calm and nonchalant as you can be when a fellow eight foot six in height with one eye bunged up and the other behaving like an oxyacetylene blowpipe is glaring at you.

"Yes, sir," said Spode, "it'll be chokey for you."

And he was going on to say that he would derive great pleasure from coming on visiting days and making faces at me through the bars, when Pop Bassett returned.

But a very different Bassett from the fizzy rejoicer who had exited so short a while before. Then he had been all buck and beans, as any father would have been whose daughter was not going to marry Gussie Fink-Nottle. Now his face was drawn and his general demeanor that of an incautious luncher who discovers when there is no time to draw back that he has swallowed a rather too elderly oyster.

"Madeline tells me," he began. Then he saw Spode's eye and broke off. It was the sort of eye which, even if you have a lot on your mind, you can't help noticing. "Good gracious, Roderick," he said, "did you have a fall?"

"Fall, my foot," said Spode; "I was socked by a curate."

"Good heavens! What curate?"

"There's only one in these parts, isn't there?"

"You mean you were assaulted by Mr. Pinker? You astound me, Roderick."

Spode spoke with genuine feeling.

"Not half as much as he astounded *me*. He was more or less of a revelation to me, I don't mind telling you, because I didn't know curates had left hooks like that. He's got a knack of feinting you off balance and then coming in with a sort of corkscrew punch which it's impossible not to admire. I must get him to teach it to me some time."

"You speak as though you bore him no animosity."

"Of course I don't. A very pleasant little scrap with no ill feeling on either side. I've nothing against Pinker. The one I've got it in for is the cook. She beaned me with a china basin. From behind, of all unsporting things. If you'll excuse me, I'll go and have a word with that cook."

He was so obviously looking forward to telling Emerald Stoker what he thought of her that it gave me quite a pang to have to break it to him that his errand would be bootless.

"You can't," I pointed out. "She is no longer with us."

"Don't be an ass. She's in the kitchen, isn't she?"

"I'm sorry, no. She's eloped with Gussie Fink-Nottle. A wedding has been arranged and will take place as soon as the Archbish of Canterbury lets him have a special license."

Spode reeled. He had only one eye to stare at me with, but he got all the mileage out of it that was possible.

"Is that true?"

"Absolutely."

"Well, that makes up for everything. If Madeline's back in circulation . . . Thank you for telling me, Wooster, old chap."

"Don't mention it, Spode, old man, or, rather, Lord Sidcup, old man."

For the first time, Pop Bassett appeared to become aware that the slight, distinguished-looking young fellow standing on one leg by the sofa was Bertram.

"Mr. Wooster," he said. Then he stopped, swallowed once or twice, and groped his way to the table where the drinks were. His manner was feverish. Having passed a liberal snootful down the hatch, he was able to resume. "I have just seen Madeline."

"Oh yes?" I said courteously. "How is she?"

"Off her head, in my opinion. She says she is going to marry you."

Well, I had more or less steeled myself to something along

these lines, so except for quivering like a stricken blanc-mange and letting my lower jaw fall perhaps six inches I betrayed no sign of discomposure, in which respect I differed radically from Spode, who reeled for the second time and uttered a cry like that of a cinnamon bear that has stubbed its toe on a passing rock.

"You're joking!"

Pop Bassett shook his head regretfully. His face was haggard.

"I wish I were, Roderick. I am not surprised that you are upset. I feel the same myself. I am distraught. I can see no light on the horizon. When she told me, it was as if I had been struck by a thunderbolt."

Spode was staring at me, aghast. Even now, it seemed, he was unable to take in the full horror of the situation. There was incredulity in his one good eye.

"But she can't marry *that!*"

"She seems resolved to."

"But he's worse than that fish-faced blighter."

"I agree with you. Far worse. No comparison."

"I'll go and talk to her," said Spode, and left us before I could express my resentment at being called *that*.

It was perhaps fortunate that only half a minute later Stiffy and Stinker entered, for if I had been left alone with Pop Bassett, I would have been hard put to it to hit on a topic of conversation calculated to interest, elevate, and amuse.

CHAPTER

NINETEEN

STINKER'S NOSE, as was only to be expected, had swollen a good deal since last heard from, but he seemed in excellent spirits, and Stiffy couldn't have been merrier and brighter. Both were obviously thinking in terms of the happy ending, and my heart bled freely for the unfortunate young slobs. I had observed Pop Bassett closely while Spode was telling him about Stinker's left hook, and what I had read on his countenance had not been encouraging.

These patrons of livings with vicarages to bestow always hold rather rigid views as regards the qualifications they demand from the curates they are thinking of promoting to fields of higher activity, and left hooks, however adroit, are not among them. If Pop Bassett had been a fight promoter on the lookout for talent and Stinker a promising novice anxious to be put on his next program for a six-round preliminary bout, he would no doubt have gazed on him with a kindly eye. As it was, the eye he was now directing at him was as cold and bleak as if my old crony had been standing before him in the dock, charged with having moved pigs without a permit or failed to abate a smoky chimney. I could see trouble looming, and I wouldn't have risked a bet on the happy e. even at the most liberal odds.

The stickiness of the atmosphere, so patent to my keener sense, had not communicated itself to Stiffy. No voice was whispering in her ear that she was about to be let down with a thud which would jar her to the back teeth. She was all smiles and viv-whatever-the-word is, plainly convinced that the signing on the dotted line was now a mere formality.

"Here we are, Uncle Watkyn," she said, beaming freely.

"So I see."

"I've brought Harold."

"So I perceive."

"We've talked it over, and we think we ought to have the thing embodied in the form of a letter."

Pop Bassett's eye grew colder and bleaker, and the feeling I had that we were all back in Bosher Street Police Court deepened. Nothing, it seemed to me, was needed to complete the illusion except a magistrate's clerk with a cold in the head, a fug you could cut with a knife, and a few young barristers hanging about hoping for dock briefs.

"I fear I do not understand you," he said.

"Oh, come, Uncle Watkyn, you know you're brighter than that. I'm talking about Harold's vicarage."

"I was not aware that Mr. Pinker had a vicarage."

"The one you're going to give him, I mean."

"Oh?" said Pop Bassett, and I have seldom heard an "Oh?" that had a nastier sound. "I have just seen Roderick," he added, getting down to the *res*.

[170]

At the mention of Spode's name Stiffy giggled, and I could have told her it was a mistake. There is a time for girlish frivolity and a time when it is misplaced. It had not escaped my notice that Pop Bassett had begun to swell like one of those curious circular fish you catch down in Florida, and in addition to this he was rumbling as I imagine volcanos do before starting in on the neighboring householders and making them wish they had settled elsewhere.

But even now Stiffy seemed to have no sense of impending doom. She uttered another silvery laugh. I've noticed this slowness in getting hep to atmospheric conditions in other girls. The young of the gentler sex never appear to realize that there are moments when the last thing required by their audience is the silvery laugh.

"I'll bet he had a shiner."

"I beg your pardon?"

"Was his eye black?"

"It was."

"I thought it would be. Harold's strength is as the strength of ten, because his heart is pure. Well, how about that embodying letter? I have a fountain pen. Let's get the show on the road."

I was expecting Pop Bassett to give an impersonation of a bomb falling on an ammunition dump, but he didn't. Instead, he continued to exhibit that sort of chilly stiffness which you see in magistrates when they're fining people five quid for boyish peccadilloes.

"You appear to be under a misapprehension, Stephanie," he said in the metallic voice he had once used when addressing the prisoner Wooster. "I have no intention of entrusting Mr. Pinker with a vicarage."

Stiffy took it big. She shook from windswept hairdo to shoe sole, and if she hadn't clutched at Stinker's arm might have taken a toss. One could understand her emotion. She had been coasting along, confident that she had it made, and suddenly out of a blue and smiling sky these words of doom. No doubt it was the suddenness and unexpectedness of the wallop that unmanned her, if you can call it unmanning when it happens to a girl. I suppose she was feeling very much as Spode had felt when Emerald Stoker's basin had connected with his occiput. Her eyes bulged, and her voice came out in a passionate squeak.

"But, Uncle Watkyn! You promised!"

I could have told her she was wasting her breath trying to appeal to the old buzzard's better feelings, because magistrates, even when ex, don't have any. The tremolo in her voice might have been expected to melt what is usually called a heart of stone, but it had no more effect on Pop Bassett than the chirping of the household canary.

"Provisionally only," he said. " I was not aware, when I did so, that Mr. Pinker had brutally assaulted Roderick."

At these words Stinker, who had been listening to the exchanges in a rigid sort of way, creating the illusion that he had been stuffed by a good taxidermist, came suddenly to life, though, as all he did was make a sound like the last drops of water going out of a bathtub, it was hardly worth the trouble and expense. He succeeded, however, in attracting Pop Bassett's attention, and the latter gave him the eye.

"Yes, Mr. Pinker?"

It was a moment or two before Stinker followed up the gurgling noise with speech. And even then it wasn't much in the way of speech. He said: "I—er—He—er—"

"Proceed, Mr. Pinker."

"It was—I mean it wasn't—"

"If you could make yourself a little plainer, Mr. Pinker, it would be of great assistance to our investigations into the matter under discussion. I must confess to finding you far from lucid."

It was the type of crack he had been accustomed in the old Bosher Street days to seeing in print with "laughter" after it in brackets, but on this occasion it fell flatter than a Dover sole. It didn't get a snicker out of me, or out of Stinker, who merely knocked over a small china ornament and turned a deeper vermilion, while Stiffy came back at him in great shape.

"There's no need to talk like a magistrate, Uncle Watkyn."

"I beg your pardon?"

"In fact, it would be better if you stopped talking at all and let me explain. What Harold's trying to tell you is that he didn't brutally assault Roderick; Roderick brutally assaulted him."

"Indeed? That was not the way I heard the story."

"Well, it's the way it happened."

"I am perfectly willing to hear your version of the deplorable incident."

"All right, then. Here it comes. Harold was cooing to Roderick like a turtledove, and Roderick suddenly hauled off and plugged him squarely on the beezer. If you don't believe me, take a look at it. The poor angel spouted blood like a Versailles fountain. Well, what would you have expected Harold to do? Turn the other nose?"

"I would have expected him to remember his position as a clerk in holy orders. He should have complained to me, and I would have seen to it that Roderick made ample apology."

A sound like the shot heard round the world rang through the room. It was Stiffy snorting.

"Apology!" she cried, having got the snort out of her system. "What's the good of apologies? Harold took the only possible course. He sailed in and laid Roderick out cold, as anyone would have done in his place."

"Anyone who had not his cloth to think of."

"For goodness' sake, Uncle Watkyn, a fellow can't be thinking of cloth all the time. It was an emergency. Roderick was murdering Gussie Fink-Nottle."

"And Mr. Pinker *stopped* him? Great heavens!"

There was a pause while Pop Bassett struggled with his feelings. Then Stiffy, as Stinker had done with Spode, had a shot at the honeyed word. She had spoken of Stinker cooing to Spode like a turtledove, and if memory served me aright that was just how he had cooed, and it was of a cooing turtledove that she now reminded me. Like most girls, she can always get a melting note into her voice if she thinks there's any percentage to be derived from it.

"It's not like you, Uncle Watkyn, to go back on your solemn promise."

I could have corrected her there. I would have thought it was just like him.

"I can't believe it's really you who's doing this cruel thing to me. It's so unlike you. You have always been so kind to me. You have made me love and respect you. I have come to look on you as a second father. Don't louse the whole thing up now."

A powerful plea, which with any other man would undoubtedly have brought home the bacon. With Pop Bassett it didn't get to first base. He had been looking like a man with no bowels—of compassion, I mean of course—and he went on looking like one.

"If by that peculiar expression you intend to imply that you are expecting me to change my mind and give Mr. Pinker this vicarage, I must disappoint you. I shall do no such thing. I consider that he has shown himself unfit to be a vicar, and I am surprised that after what has occurred he can reconcile it with his conscience to continue his duties as a curate."

[174]

Strong stuff, of course, and it drew from Stinker what may have been a hollow groan or may have been a hiccup. I myself looked coldly at the old egg, and I rather think I curled my lip, though I should say it was very doubtful if he noticed my scorn, for his attention was earmarked for Stiffy. She had turned almost as scarlet as Stinker, and I heard a distinct click as her front teeth met. It was through these teeth (clenched) that she spoke.

"So that's how you feel about it?"

"It is."

"Your decision is final?"

"Quite final."

"Nothing will move you?"

"Nothing."

"I see," said Stiffy, having chewed the lower lip for a space in silence. "Well, you'll be sorry."

"I disagree with you."

"You will. Just wait. Bitter remorse is coming to you, Uncle Watkyn. Never underestimate the power of a woman," said Stiffy, and with a choking sob—though there again it may have been a hiccup—she rushed from the room.

She had scarcely left us when Butterfield entered, and Pop Bassett eyed him with the ill-concealed petulance with which men of testy habit eye butlers who butt in at the wrong moment.

"Yes, Butterfield? What is it, what is it?"

"Constable Oates desires a word with you, sir."

"Who?"

"Police Constable Oates, sir."

"What does he want?"

"I gather that he has a clue to the identity of the boy who threw a hard-boiled egg at you, sir."

The words acted on Pop Bassett as I'm told the sound of

bugles acts on war-horses, not that I've ever seen a war-horse. His whole demeanor changed in a flash. His face lit up, and there came into it the sort of look you see on the faces of bloodhounds when they settle down to the trail. He didn't actually say "Whoopee!" but that was probably because the expression was not familiar to him. He was out of the room in a matter of seconds, Butterfield lying some lengths behind, and Stinker, who had been replacing a framed photograph which he had knocked off a neighboring table, addressed me in what you might call a hushed voice.

"I say, Bertie, what do you think Stiffy meant when she said that?"

I, too, had been speculating as to what the young pipsqueak had had in mind. A sinister thing to say, it seemed to me. Those words "just wait" had had an ominous ring. I weighed his question gravely.

"Difficult to decide," I said. "It may be one thing or it may be another."

"She has such an impulsive nature."

"Very impulsive."

"It makes me uneasy."

"Why you? Pop B's the one who ought to be feeling uneasy. Knowing her as I do, if I were in his place——"

The sentence I had begun would, if it had come to fruition, have concluded with the words "I'd pack a few necessaries in a suitcase and go to Australia," but as I was about to utter them I chanced to glance out of the window and they froze on my lips.

The window looked on the drive, and from where I was standing I got a good view of the front steps, and when I saw what was coming up those front steps, my heart leaped from its base.

It was Plank. There was no mistaking that square, tanned

face and that purposeful walk of his. And when I reflected that in about a couple of ticks Butterfield would be showing him into the drawing room where I stood and we would meet once more, I confess that I was momentarily at a loss to know how to proceed.

My first thought was to wait till he had got through the front door and then nip out of the window, which was conveniently open. That, I felt, was what Napoleon would have done. And I was just about to get the show on the road, as Stiffy would have said, when I saw the dog Bartholomew come sauntering along, and I knew that I would be compelled to revise my strategy from the bottom up. You can't go climbing out of windows under the eyes of an Aberdeen terrier so prone as Bartholomew was always to think the worst. In due season, no doubt, he would learn that what he had taken for a burglar escaping with the swag had been in reality a harmless guest of the house and would be all apologies, but by that time my lower slopes would be as full of holes as a Swiss cheese.

Falling back on my second line of defense, I slid behind the sofa with a muttered "Not a word to a soul, Stinker. Chap I don't want to meet," and was nestling there like a turtle in its shell, when the door opened.

CHAPTER
TWENTY

IT'S PRETTY generally recognized at the Drones Club and elsewhere that Bertram Wooster is a man who knows how to keep the chin up and the upper lip stiff, no matter how rough the going may be. Beneath the bludgeonings of Fate, his head is bloody but unbowed, as the fellow said. In a word, he can take it.

But I must admit that as I crouched in my haven of refuge I found myself chafing not a little. Life at Totleigh Towers, as I mentioned earlier, had got me down. There seemed no way of staying put in the darned house. One was either soaring like an eagle on to the top of chests or whizzing down behind sofas like a diving duck, and apart from the hustle and bustle of it all that sort of thing wounds the spirit and does no good to the trouser crease. And so, as I say, I chafed.

I was becoming increasingly bitter about this man Plank and the tendency he seemed to be developing of haunting me like a family specter. I couldn't imagine what he was doing here. Whatever the faults of Totleigh Towers, I had supposed that, when there, one would at least be free from his society. He had an excellent home in Hockley-cum-Meston, and one sought in vain for an explanation of why the hell he didn't stay in it.

My disapproval extended to the personnel of the various native tribes he had encountered in the course of his ex-plorations. On his own showing, he had for years been horn-ing in uninvited on the aborigines of Brazil, the Congo, and elsewhere, and not one of them apparently had had the en-terprise to get after him with a spear or to say it with poisoned darts from the family blowpipe. And these were fellows who called themselves savages. Savages, forsooth! The savages in the books I used to read in my childhood would have had him in the obituary column before he could say "What ho," but with the ones you get nowadays it's all slackness and laissez-faire. Can't be bothered. Leave it to somebody else. Let George do it. One sometimes wonders what the world's coming to.

From where I sat, my range of vision was necessarily a bit restricted, but I was able to see a pair of Empire-building brogue shoes, so I assumed that when the door had opened it was Butterfield showing him in, and this sur-mise was confirmed a moment later when he spoke. His was a voice which, once heard, lingers in the memory.

"Afternoon," he said.

"Good afternoon," said Stinker.

"Warm day."

"Very warm."

"What's been going on here? What are all those tents and swings and things in the park?"

Stinker explained that the annual school treat had only just concluded, and Plank expressed his gratification at having missed it. School treats, he said, were dashed dangerous things, always to be avoided by the shrewd, as they were only too apt to include competitions for bonny babies.

"Did you have a competition for bonny babies?"

"Yes, we did, as a matter of fact. The mothers always insist on it."

"The mothers are the ones you want to watch out for," said Plank. "I'm not saying the little beasts aren't bad enough themselves, dribbling out of the side of their mouths at you and all that sort of thing, but it's the mothers who constitute the really grave peril. Look," he said, and I think he must at this point have pulled up a trouser leg. "See that scar on my calf? That's what I got in Peru once for being fool enough to let myself be talked into judging a competition for bonny babies. The mother of one of the Honorably Mentioneds spiked me in the leg with a native dagger as I was stepping down from the judge's stand after making my speech. Hurt like sin, I can assure you, and still gives me a twinge when the weather's wet. Fellow I know is fond of saying that the hand that rocks the cradle rules the world. Whether this is so or not I couldn't tell you, but it certainly knows how to handle a Peruvian dagger."

I found myself revising to some extent the rather austere opinion I had formed of the slackness and lack of ginger of the modern native. The males might have lost their grip in recent years, but the female element, it seemed, still had the right stuff in them, though of course, where somebody like Plank is concerned, a stab in the fleshy part of the leg is only a step in the right direction, merely scratching the surface as you might say.

Plank continued chatty. "You live in these parts?" he said.

"Yes, I live in the village."

"Totleigh?"

"Yes."

"Don't run a Rugger club in Totleigh, do you?"

Stinker replied in the negative. The Totleigh-in-the-Wold athletes, he said, preferred the Association code, and Plank, probably shuddering, said, "Good God!"

"You ever played Rugger?"

"A little."

"You should take it up seriously. No finer sport. I'm trying to make the Hockley-cum-Meston team the talk of Gloucestershire. I coach the boys daily, and they're coming along very nicely, very nicely indeed. What I need is a good prop forward."

What he got was Pop Bassett, who came bustling in at this moment. He Good-afternoon-Plank-ed, and Plank responded in suitable terms.

"Very nice of you to look me up, Plank," said Pop. "Will you have something to drink?"

"Ah," said Plank, and you could see that he meant it.

"I would ask you to stay to dinner, but unfortunately one of my guests has eloped with the cook."

"Dashed sensible of him, if he was going to elope with anyone. Very hard to find these days, cooks."

"It has of course completely disorganized our domestic arrangements. Neither my daughter nor my niece is capable of preparing even the simplest meal."

"You'll have to go to the pub."

"It seems the only solution."

"If you were in West Africa, you could drop in and take potluck with a native chief."

"I am not in West Africa," said Pop Bassett, speaking, I thought, a little testily, and I could understand him feeling a bit miffed. It's always annoying when you're up against it and people tell you what a jolly time you could be having if you weren't and how topping everything would be if you were somewhere where you aren't.

"I dined out a good deal in West Africa," said Plank. "Capital dinners some of those fellows used to give me, I remember, though there was always the drawback that you could never be sure the main dish wasn't one of their wives' relations, broiled over a slow fire and disguised in some native sauce. Took the edge off your appetite, unless you were feeling particularly peckish."

"So I would be disposed to imagine."

"All a matter of taste, of course."

"Quite. Was there something you particularly wished to see me about, Plank?"

"No, nothing that I can think of."

"Then if you will excuse me, I will be getting back to Madeline."

"Who's Madeline?"

"My daughter. Your arrival interrupted me in a serious talk I was having with her."

"Something wrong with the girl?"

"Something extremely wrong. She is contemplating making a disastrous marriage."

"All marriages are disastrous," said Plank, who gave one the impression, reading between the lines, that he was a bachelor. "They lead to bonny babies, and bonny babies lead to bonny-baby competitions. I was telling this gentleman here of an experience I had in Peru and showing him the scar on my leg, the direct result of being ass enough to judge one of these competitions. Would you care to see the scar on my leg?"

"Some other time, perhaps."

"Any time that suits you. Why is this marriage you say she's contemplating so disastrous?"

[182]

"Because Mr. Wooster is not a suitable husband for her."

"Who's Mr. Wooster?"

"The man she wishes to marry. A typical young wastrel of the type so common nowadays."

"I used to know a fellow called Wooster, but I don't suppose it can be the same chap, because my Wooster was eaten by a crocodile on the Zambesi the other day, which rather rules him out. All right, Bassett, you pop back to the girl and tell her from me that if she's going to start marrying every Tom, Dick, and Harry she comes across, she ought to have her head examined. If she'd seen as many native chiefs' wives as I have, she wouldn't be wanting to make such an ass of herself. Dickens of a life they lead, those women. Nothing to do but grind maize meal and have bonny babies. Right ho, Bassett, don't let me keep you."

There came the sound of a closing door as Pop Bassett sped on his way, and Plank turned his attention to Stinker. He said: "I didn't tell that old ass, because I didn't want him sticking around in here talking his head off, but as a matter of fact I did come about something special. Do you happen to know where I can find a chap called Pinker?"

"My name's Pinker."

"Are you sure? I thought Bassett said it was Wooster."

"No, Wooster's the one who's going to marry Sir Watkyn's daughter."

"So he is. It all comes back to me now. I wonder if you can be the fellow I want. The Pinker I'm after is a curate."

"I'm a curate."

"You are? Yes, by Jove, you're perfectly right. I see your collar buttons at the back. You're not H. P. Pinker by any chance?"

"Yes."

"Prop forward for Oxford and England a few years ago?"

[183]

"Yes."

"Well, would you be interested in becoming a vicar?"

There was a crashing sound, and I knew that Stinker in his emotion must have upset his customary table. After a while he said in a husky voice that the one thing he wanted was to get his hooks on a vicarage or words to that effect, and Plank said he was glad to hear it.

"My chap at Hockley-cum-Meston is downing tools now that his ninetieth birthday is approaching, and I've been scouring the countryside for a spare. Extraordinarily difficult the quest has been, because what I wanted was a vicar who was a good prop forward, and it isn't often you find a parson who knows one end of a football from the other. I've never seen you play, I'm sorry to say, because I've been abroad so much, but with your record you must obviously be outstanding. So you can take up your duties as soon as old Bellamy goes into storage. When I get home, I'll embody the thing in the form of a letter."

Stinker said he didn't know how to thank him, and Plank said that was all right, no need of any thanks.

"I'm the one who ought to be grateful. We're all right at halfback and three-quarters, but we lost to Upper Bleaching last year simply because our prop forward proved a broken reed. This year we'll show 'em. Amazing bit of luck finding you, and I could never have done it if it hadn't been for a friend of mine, a Chief Inspector Witherspoon of Scotland Yard. He phoned me just now and told me you were to be found at Totleigh-in-the-Wold. He said if I called at Totleigh Towers, they would give me your address. Extraordinary how these Scotland Yard fellows nose things out. The result of years of practice, I suppose. What was that noise?"

Stinker said he had heard nothing.

"Sort of gasping noise. Seemed to come from behind that sofa. Take a look."

I was aware for a moment of Stinker's face peering down at me; then he turned away.

"There's nothing behind the sofa," he said, very decently imperiling his immortal soul by falsifying the facts on behalf of a pal.

"Thought it might be a dog being sick," said Plank.

And I suppose it had sounded rather like that. The revelation of Jeeves' black treachery had shaken me to my foundations, causing me to forget that in the existing circs silence was golden. A silly thing to do, of course, to gasp like that, but, dash it, if for years you have nursed a gentleman's personal gentleman in your bosom and out of a blue sky you find that he has deliberately sicced Brazilian explorers on to you, I maintain that you're fully entitled to behave like a dog in the throes of nausea. I could make nothing of his scurvy conduct and was so stunned that for a minute or two I lost the thread of the conversation. When the mists cleared, Plank was speaking, and the subject had been changed.

"I wonder how Bassett is getting on with that daughter of his. Do you know anything of this chap Wooster?"

"He's one of my best friends."

"Bassett doesn't seem too fond of him."

"No."

"Ah well, we all have our likes and dislikes. Which of the two girls is this Madeline he was speaking of? I've never met them, but I've seen them around. Is she the little squirt with the large blue eyes?"

I should imagine Stinker didn't care overmuch for hearing his loved one described as a little squirt, though reason must have told him that that was precisely what she was, but he replied without heat.

"No, that's Sir Watkyn's niece, Stephanie Byng."

"Byng? Now why does that name seem to ring a bell? Oh yes, of course. Old Johnny Byng, who was with me on one of my expeditions. Red-haired fellow; haven't seen him for years. He was bitten by a puma, poor chap, and they tell me he still hesitates in a rather noticeable manner before sitting down. Stephanie Byng, eh? You know her, of course?"

"Very well."

"Nice girl?"

"That's how she seems to me, and if you don't mind, I'll be going and telling her the good news."

"What good news?"

"About the vicarage."

"Oh, ah, yes. You think she'll be interested?"

"I'm sure she will. We're going to be married."

"Good God! No chance of getting out of it?"

"I don't want to get out of it."

"Amazing! I once hitchhiked all the way from Johannesburg to Cape Town to avoid getting married, and here you are seeming quite pleased at the prospect. Oh well, no accounting for tastes. All right, you run along. And I suppose I'd better have a word with Bassett before I leave. Fellow bores me stiff, but one has to be civil."

The door closed and silence fell, and after waiting a few minutes, just in case, I felt it was safe to surface. And I had just done so and was limbering up the limbs, which had become somewhat cramped, when the door opened and Jeeves came in carrying a tray.

CHAPTER
TWENTY-ONE

"GOOD EVENING, sir," he said. "Would you care for an appetizer? I was obliging Mr. Butterfield by bringing them. He is engaged at the moment in listening at the door of the room where Sir Watkyn is in conference with Miss Bassett. He tells me he is compiling his memoirs and never misses an opportunity of gathering suitable material."

I gave the man one of my looks. My face was cold and hard, like a school treat egg. I can't remember a time when I've been fuller of righteous indignation.

"What I want, Jeeves, is not a slab of wet bread with a dead sardine on it—"

"Anchovy, sir."

"Or anchovy. I am in no mood to split straws. I require an explanation, and a categorical one, at that."

"Sir?"

"You can't evade the issue by saying 'Sir?' Answer me this, Jeeves, with a simple yes or no. Why did you tell Plank to come to Totleigh Towers?"

I thought the query would crumple him up like a damp sock, but he didn't so much as shuffle a foot.

"My heart was melted by Miss Byng's tale of her misfortunes, sir. I chanced to encounter the young lady and found her in a state of considerable despondency as the result of Sir Watkyn's refusal to bestow a vicarage on Mr. Pinker. I perceived immediately that it was within my power to alleviate her distress. I had learned at the post office at Hockley-cum-Meston that the incumbent there was retiring shortly, and being cognizant of Major Plank's desire to strengthen the Hockley-cum-Meston forward line, I felt that it would be an excellent idea to place him in communication with Mr. Pinker. In order to be in a position to marry Miss Byng, Mr. Pinker requires a vicarage, and in order to compete successfully with rival villages in the football arena, Major Plank is in need of a vicar with Mr. Pinker's wide experience as a prop forward. Their interests appeared to me to be identical."

"Well, it worked all right. Stinker has clicked."

"He is to succeed Mr. Bellamy as incumbent at Hockley-cum-Meston?"

"As soon as Bellamy calls it a day."

"I am very happy to hear it, sir."

I didn't reply for a while, being obliged to attend to a sudden touch of cramp. This ironed out, I said, still icy: "You may be happy, but I haven't been for the last quarter of an hour or so, nestling behind the sofa and expecting Plank at any moment to unmask me. It didn't occur to you to envisage what would happen if he met me?"

"I was sure that your keen intelligence would enable you

to find a means of avoiding him, sir, as indeed it did. You concealed yourself behind the sofa?"

"On all fours."

"A very shrewd maneuver on your part, if I may say so, sir. It showed a resource and swiftness of thought which it would be difficult to overpraise."

My iciness melted. It is not too much to say that I was mollified. It's not often that I'm given the old oil in this fashion, most of my circle, notably my Aunt Agatha, being more prone to the slam than the rave. And it was only after I had been savoring that "keen intelligence" gag, if savoring is the word I want, for some moments that I suddenly remembered that marriage with Madeline Bassett loomed ahead, and I gave a start so visible that he asked me if I was feeling unwell.

I shook the loaf.

"Physically, no, Jeeves. Spiritually, yes."

"I do not quite understand you, sir."

"Well, here is the news, and this is Bertram Wooster reading it. I'm going to be married."

"Indeed, sir?"

"Yes, Jeeves, married. The banns are as good as up."

"Would it be taking a liberty if I were to ask—"

"Who to? You don't need to ask. Gussie Fink-Nottle has eloped with Emerald Stoker, thus creating a . . . what is it?"

"Would vacuum be the word you are seeking, sir?"

"That's right. A vacuum which I shall have to fill. Unless you can think of some way of getting me out of it."

"I will devote considerable thought to the matter, sir."

"Thank you, Jeeves," I said, and would have spoken further, but at this moment I saw the door opening and speechlessness supervened. But it wasn't, as I had feared, Plank; it was only Stiffy.

"Hullo, you two," she said. "I'm looking for Harold."

I could see at a g. that Jeeves had been right in describing her demeanor as despondent. The brow was clouded and the general appearance that of an overwrought soul. I was glad to be in a position to inject a little sunshine into her life. Pigeonholing my own troubles for future reference, I said: "He's looking for you. He has a strange story to relate. You know Plank?"

"What about him?"

"I'll tell you what about him. Plank to you hitherto has been merely a shadowy figure who hangs out at Hockley-cum-Meston and sells black amber statuettes to people, but he has another side to him."

She betrayed a certain impatience.

"If you think I'm interested in Plank—"

"Aren't you?"

"No, I'm not."

"You will be. He has, as I was saying, another side to him. He is a landed proprietor with vicarages in his gift, and, to cut a long story down to a short-short, as one always likes to do when possible, he has just given one to Stinker."

I had been right in supposing that the information would have a marked effect on her dark mood. I have never actually seen a corpse spring from its bier and start being the life and soul of the party, but I should imagine that its deportment would closely resemble that of this young Byng as the impact of my words came home to her. A sudden light shot into her eyes, which, as Plank had correctly said, were large and blue, and an ecstatic "Well, Lord love a duck!" escaped her. Then doubts seemed to creep in, for the eyes clouded over again.

"Is this true?"

"Absolutely official."

"You aren't pulling my leg?"

I drew myself up rather haughtily.

"I wouldn't dream of pulling your leg. Do you think Bertram Wooster is the sort of chap who thinks it funny to raise people's hopes, only to . . . what, Jeeves?"

"Dash them to the ground, sir."

"Thank you, Jeeves."

"Not at all, sir."

"You may take this information as coming straight from the mouth of the stable cat. I was present when the deal went through. Behind the sofa, but present."

She still seemed at a loss.

"But I don't understand. Plank has never met Harold."

"Jeeves brought them together."

"Did you, Jeeves?"

"Yes, miss."

"At-a-boy!"

"Thank you, miss."

"And he's really given Harold a vicarage?"

"The vicarage of Hockley-cum-Meston. He's embodying it in the form of a letter tonight. At the moment there's a vicar still vicking, but he's infirm and old and wants to turn it up as soon as they can put on an understudy. The way things look, I should imagine that we shall be able to unleash Stinker on the Hockley-cum-Meston souls in the course of the next few days."

My simple words and earnest manner had resolved the last of her doubts. The misgivings she may have had as to whether this was the real ginger vanished. Her eyes shone more like twin stars than anything, and she uttered animal cries and danced a few dance steps. Presently she paused and put a question.

"What's Plank like?"

"How do you mean, what's he like?"

"He hasn't a beard, has he?"

"No, no beard."

"That's good, because I want to kiss him, and if he had a beard, it would give me pause."

"Dismiss the notion," I urged, for Plank's psychology was an open book to me. The whole trend of that confirmed bachelor's conversation had left me with the impression that he would find it infinitely preferable to be spiked in the leg with a native dagger than to have popsies covering his upturned face with kisses. "He'd have a fit."

"Well, I must kiss somebody. Shall I kiss you, Jeeves?"

"No, thank you, miss."

"You, Bertie?"

"I'd rather you didn't."

"Then I've a good mind to go and kiss Uncle Watkyn, louse of the first water though he has recently shown himself."

"How do you mean, recently?"

"And having kissed him I shall tell him the news and taunt him vigorously with having let a good thing get away from him. I shall tell him that when he declined to avail himself of Harold's services he was like the Indian."

I did not get her drift.

"What Indian?"

"The base one my governesses used to make me read about, the poor simp whose hand . . . How does it go, Jeeves?"

"Threw a pearl away richer than all his tribe, miss."

"That's right. And I shall tell him I hope the vicar he does get will be a weed of a man who has a chronic cold in the head and bleats. Oh, by the way, talking of Uncle Watkyn reminds me. I shan't have any use for this now."

And so speaking she produced the black amber eyesore from the recesses of her costume like a conjurer taking a rabbit out of a hat.

CHAPTER
TWENTY-TWO

IT WAS as if she had suddenly exhibited a snake of the lowest order. I gazed at the thing, appalled. It needed but this to put the frosting on the cake.

"Where did you get that?" I asked in a voice that was low and trembled.

"I pinched it."

"What on earth did you do that for?"

"Perfectly simple. The idea was to go to Uncle Watkyn and tell him he wouldn't get it back unless he did the square thing by Harold. Power politics, don't they call it, Jeeves?"

"Or blackmail, miss."

"Yes, or blackmail, I suppose. But you can't be too nice in your methods when you're dealing with the Uncle Watkyns of this world. But now that Plank has eased the situation and made our paths straight, of course I shan't need it, and I suppose the shrewd thing is to return it to store before its absence is noted. Go and put it in the collection room, Bertie. Here's the key."

I recoiled as if she had offered me the dog Bartholomew. Priding myself as I do on being a *preux chevalier*, I like to oblige the delicately nurtured when it's feasible, but there are moments when only a *nolle prosequi* will serve, and I recognized this as one of them. The thought of making the perilous passage she was suggesting gave me goose pimples.

"I'm not going near the ruddy collection room. With my luck, I'd find your Uncle Watkyn there, arm in arm with Spode, and it wouldn't be too easy to explain what I was doing there and how I'd got in. Besides, I can't go roaming about the place with Plank on the premises."

She laughed one of those silvery ones, a practice to which, as I have indicated, she was far too much addicted.

"Jeeves told me about you and Plank. Very funny."

"I'm glad you think so. We personally were not amused."

Jeeves, as always, found the way.

"If you will give the object to me, miss, I will see that it is restored to its place."

"Thank you, Jeeves. Well, goodbye all. I'm off to find Harold," said Stiffy, and she withdrew, dancing on the tips of her toes.

I shrugged a shoulder.

"Women, Jeeves!"

"Yes, sir."

"What a sex!"

"Yes, sir."

"Do you remember something I said to you about Stiffy on our previous visit to Totleigh Towers?"

"Not at the moment, no, sir."

"It was on the occasion when she landed me with Police Constable Oates' helmet just as my room was about to be searched by Pop Bassett and his minions. Dipping into the future, I pointed out that Stiffy, who is pure padded cell from the foundations up, was planning to marry the Rev. H. P. Pinker, himself as pronounced a goop as ever preached about the Hivites and Hittites, and I speculated, if you recall, as to what their offspring, if any, would be like."

"Ah yes, sir, I recollect now."

"Would they, I asked myself, inherit the combined loopiness of two such parents?"

"Yes, sir, you were particularly concerned, I recall, for the well-being of the nurses, governesses, private-school masters, and public-school masters who would assume the charge of them."

"Little knowing that they were coming up against something hotter than mustard. Exactly. The thought still weighs heavy upon me. However, we haven't leisure to go into the subject now. You'd better take that ghastly object back where it belongs without delay."

"Yes, sir. If it were done when 'twere done, then 'twere well it were done quickly," he said, making for the door, and I thought, as I had so often thought before, how neatly he put these things.

It seemed to me that the time had now come to adopt the strategy which I had had in mind right at the beginning—viz., to make my getaway via the window. With Plank at large in the house and likely at any moment to come winging back to where the drinks were, safety could be obtained only by making for some distant yew alley or rhododendron walk and remaining ensconced there till he had blown over. I hastened to the window, accordingly, and picture my chagrin and dismay on finding that Bartholomew, instead of continuing his stroll, had decided to take a siesta on the grass immediately below. I had actually got one leg over the sill before he was drawn to my attention. In another half jiffy I should have dropped on him as the gentle rain from heaven upon the spot beneath.

I had no difficulty in recognizing the situation as what the French call an *impasse,* and as I stood pondering what to do for the best, footsteps sounded without, and feeling that 'twere well it were done quickly I made for the sofa once more, lowering my previous record by perhaps a split second.

I was surprised, as I lay nestling in my little nook, by the complete absence of dialogue that ensued. Hitherto, all my visitors had started chatting from the moment of their entry, and it struck me as odd that I should now be entertaining a couple of deaf-mutes. Peeping cautiously out, however, I found that I had been mistaken in supposing that I had with me a brace of guests. It was Madeline alone who had blown in. She was heading for the piano, and something told me that it was her intention to sing old folk songs, a pastime to which, as I have indicated, she devoted not a little of her leisure. She was particularly given to indulgence in this nuisance when her soul had been undergoing an upheaval and required soothing, as of course it probably did at this juncture.

My fears were realized. She sang two in rapid succession, and the thought that this sort of thing would be a permanent feature of our married life chilled me to the core. I've always been what you might call allergic to old folk songs, and the older they are, the more I dislike them.

Fortunately, before she could start on a third she was interrupted. Clumping footsteps sounded, the door handle turned, heavy breathing made itself heard, and a voice said,

"Madeline!" Spode's voice, husky with emotion. "Madeline," he said, "I've been looking for you everywhere."

"Oh, Roderick! How is your eye?"

"Never mind my eye," said Spode. "I didn't come here to talk about eyes."

"They say a piece of beefsteak reduces the swelling."

"Nor about beefsteaks. Sir Watkyn has told me the awful news about you and Wooster. Is it true you're going to marry him?"

"Yes, Roderick, it is true."

"But you can't love a half-baked, half-witted ass like Wooster," said Spode, and I thought the remark extremely offensive. Pick your words more carefully, Spode, I might have said, rising and confronting him. However, for one reason and another I didn't, but continued to nestle, and I heard Madeline sigh, unless it was the draft under the sofa.

"No, Roderick, I do not love him. He does not appeal to the essential me. But I feel it is my duty to make him happy."

"Tchah!" said Spode, or something that sounded like that. "Why on earth do you want to go about making worms like Wooster happy?"

"He loves me, Roderick. You must have seen that dumb, worshiping look in his eyes as he gazes at me."

"I've something better to do than peer into Wooster's eyes. Though I can well imagine they look dumb. We've got to have this thing out, Madeline."

"I don't understand you, Roderick."

"You will."

"Ouch!"

I think on the cue "You will" he must have grabbed her by the wrist, for the word "Ouch!" had come through strong

[197]

and clear, and this suspicion was confirmed when she said he was hurting her.

"I'm sorry, sorry," said Spode. "But I refuse to allow you to ruin your life. You can't marry this man Wooster. I'm the one you're going to marry."

I was with him heart and soul, as the expression is. Nothing would ever make me really fond of Roderick Spode, but I liked the way he was talking. A little more of this, I felt, and Bertram would be released from his honorable obligations. I wished he had thought of taking this firm line earlier.

"I've loved you since you were so high."

Not being able to see him, I couldn't ascertain how high that was, but I presumed he must have been holding his hand not far from the floor. A couple of feet, would you say? About that, I suppose.

Madeline was plainly moved. I heard her gurgle.

"I know, Roderick, I know."

"You guessed my secret?"

"Yes, Roderick. How sad life is."

Spode declined to string along with her in this view.

"Not a bit of it. Life's fine. At least, it will be if you give this blighter Wooster the push and marry me."

"I have always been devoted to you, Roderick."

"Well, then?"

"Give me time to think."

"Carry on. Take all the time you need."

"I don't want to break Bertie's heart."

"Why not? Do him good."

"He loves me so dearly."

"Nonsense. I don't suppose he has ever loved anything in his life except a dry martini."

"How can you say that? Did he not come here because he found it impossible to stay away from me?"

"No, he jolly well didn't. Don't let him fool you on that point. He came here to pinch that black amber statuette of your father's."

"What!"

"That's what. In addition to being half-witted, he's a low thief."

"It can't be true!"

"Of course it's true. His uncle wants the thing for his collection. I heard him plotting with his aunt on the telephone not half an hour ago. 'It's going to be pretty hard to get away with it,' he was saying, 'but I'll do my best. I know how much Uncle Tom covets that statuette.' He's always stealing things. The very first time I met him, in an antique shop in the Brompton Road, he as near as a toucher got away with your father's umbrella."

A monstrous charge, and one which I can readily refute. He and Pop Bassett and I were, I concede, in the antique shop in the Brompton Road to which he had alluded, but the umbrella sequence was purely one of those laughable misunderstandings. Pop Bassett had left the blunt instrument propped against a seventeenth-century chair, and what caused me to take it up was the primeval instinct which makes a man without an umbrella, as I happened to be that morning, reach out unconsciously for the nearest one in sight, like a flower turning to the sun. The whole thing could have been explained in two words, but they hadn't let me say even one, and the slur had been allowed to rest on me.

"You shock me, Roderick!" said Madeline.

"Yes, I thought it would make you sit up."

"If this is really so, if Bertie is really a thief—"

"Well?"

"Naturally I will have nothing more to do with him. But I can't believe it."

[199]

"I'll go and fetch Sir Watkyn," said Spode. "Perhaps you'll believe him."

For several minutes after he had clumped out, Madeline must have stood in a reverie, for I didn't hear a sound out of her. Then the door opened, and the next thing that came across was a cough which I had no difficulty in recognizing.

CHAPTER
TWENTY-THREE

IT WAS that soft cough of Jeeves' which always reminds me
of a very old sheep clearing its throat on a distant mountain-
top. He coughed it at me, if you remember, on the occasion
when I first swam into his ken wearing the Alpine hat. It
generally signifies disapproval, but I've known it to occur
also when he's about to touch on a topic of a delicate nature.
And when he spoke, I knew that that was what he was going
to do now, for there was a sort of hushed note in his voice.

"I wonder if I might have a moment of your time, miss?"

"Of course, Jeeves."

"It is with reference to Mr. Wooster."

"Oh, yes?"

"I must begin by saying that I chanced to be passing the
door when Lord Sidcup was speaking to you and inadvert-

ently overheard his lordship's observations on the subject of Mr. Wooster. His lordship has a carrying voice. And I find myself in a somewhat equivocal position, torn between loyalty to my employer and a natural desire to do my duty as a citizen."

"I don't understand you, Jeeves," said Madeline, which made two of us.

He coughed again.

"I am anxious not to take a liberty, miss, but if I may speak frankly—"

"Please do."

"Thank you, miss. His lordship's words seemed to confirm a rumor which is circulating in the servants' hall that you are contemplating a matrimonial union with Mr. Wooster. Would it be indiscreet of me if I were to inquire if this is so?"

"Yes, Jeeves, it is quite true."

"If you will pardon me for saying so, I think you are making a mistake."

Well spoken, Jeeves, you are on the right lines, I was saying to myself, and I hoped he was going to rub it in. I waited anxiously for Madeline's reply, a little afraid that she would draw herself to her full height and dismiss him from her presence. But she didn't. She merely said again that she didn't understand him.

"If I might explain, miss. I am loath to criticize my employer, but I feel that you should know that he is a kleptomaniac."

"What!"

"Yes, miss. I had hoped to be able to preserve his little secret, as I have always done hitherto, but he has now gone to lengths which I cannot countenance. In going through his effects this afternoon I discovered this small black figure, concealed beneath his underwear."

I heard Madeline utter a sound like a dying soda-water siphon.

"But that belongs to my father!"

"If I may say so, nothing belongs to anyone if Mr. Wooster takes a fancy to it."

"Then Lord Sidcup was right?"

"Precisely, miss."

"He said Mr. Wooster tried to steal my father's umbrella."

"I heard him, and the charge was well founded. Umbrellas, jewelry, statuettes—they are all grist to Mr. Wooster's mill. I do not think he can help it. It is a form of mental illness. But whether a jury would take that view, I cannot say."

Madeline went into the soda-siphon routine once more.

"You mean he might be sent to prison?"

"It is a contingency that seems to me far from remote."

Again I felt that he was on the right lines. His trained senses told him that if there's one thing that puts a girl off marrying a chap, it is the thought that the honeymoon may be spoiled at any moment by the arrival of inspectors at the love nest, come to scoop him in for larceny. No young bride likes that sort of thing, and you can't blame her if she finds herself preferring to team up with someone like Spode, who, though a gorilla in fairly human shape, is known to keep strictly on the right side of the law. I could almost hear Madeline's thoughts turning in this direction, and I applauded Jeeves' sound grip on the psychology of the individual, as he calls it.

Of course, I could see that all this wasn't going to make my position in the Bassett home any too good, but there are times when only the surgeon's knife will serve. And I had the sustaining thought that if ever I got out from behind this sofa, I could sneak off to where my car waited champing at the bit and drive off Londonwards without stopping to say goodbye and thanks for a delightful visit. This would obviate—is it obviate?—all unpleasantness.

Madeline continued shaken.

"Oh dear, oh dear!" she said.

"Yes, miss."

"This has come as a great shock."

"I can readily appreciate it, miss."

"Have you known of this long?"

"Ever since I entered Mr. Wooster's employment."

"Oh dear, oh dear! Well, thank you, Jeeves."

"Not at all, miss."

I think Jeeves must have shimmered off after this, for silence fell and nothing happened except that my nose began to tickle. I would have given ten quid to have been able to sneeze, but this of course was outside the range of practical politics. I just crouched there, thinking of this and that, and after quite a while the door opened once more, this time to admit something in the nature of a mob scene. I could see three pairs of shoes and deduced that they were those of Spode, Pop Bassett, and Plank. Spode, it will be recalled, had gone to fetch Pop, and Plank presumably had come along for the ride, hoping no doubt for something moist at journey's end.

Spode was the first to speak, and his voice rang with the triumph that comes into the voices of suitors who have caught a dangerous rival bending.

"Here we are," he said. "I've brought Sir Watkyn to support my statement that Wooster is a low sneak thief who goes about snapping up everything that isn't nailed down. You agree, Sir Watkyn?"

"Of course I do, Roderick. It's only a month or so ago that he and that aunt of his stole my cow creamer."

"What's a cow creamer?" asked Plank.

"A silver cream jug, one of the gems of my collection."

"They got away with it, did they?"

"They did."

"Ah," said Plank. "Then in that case I think I'll have a whiskey-and-soda."

Pop Bassett was warming to his theme. His voice rose above the hissing of Plank's siphon.

"And it was only by the mercy of Providence that Wooster didn't make off with my umbrella that day in the Brompton Road. If that young man has one defect more marked than another, it is that he appears to be totally ignorant of the distinction between *meum* and *tuum*. He came up before me in my court once, I remember, charged with having stolen a policeman's helmet, and it is a lasting regret to me that I merely fined him five pounds."

"Mistaken kindness," said Spode.

"So I have always felt, Roderick. A sharper lesson might have done him all the good in the world."

"Never does to let these fellows off lightly," said Plank. "I had a servant chap in Mozambique who used to help himself to my cigars, and I foolishly overlooked it because he assured me he had got religion and everything would be quite all right from now on. And it wasn't a week later that he skipped out, taking with him a box of Havanas and my false teeth, which he sold to one of the native chiefs in the neighborhood. Cost me a case of trade gin and two strings of beads to get them back. Severity's the only thing. The iron hand. Anything else is mistaken for weakness."

Madeline gave a sob; at least it sounded like a sob.

"But, Daddy."

"Well?"

"I don't think Bertie can help himself."

"My dear child, it is precisely his habit of helping himself to everything he can lay his hands on that we are criticizing."

"I mean, he's a kleptomaniac."

"Eh? Who told you that?"

"Jeeves."

"That's odd. How did the subject come up?"

"He told me when he gave me this. He found it in Bertie's room. He was very worried about it."

There was a spot of silence—of a stunned nature, I imagine. Then Pop Bassett said "Good heavens!" and Spode said "Good Lord!" and Plank said "Why, that's that little thingummy I sold you, Bassett, isn't it?" Madeline gave another sob, and my nose began to tickle again.

"Well, this is astounding!" said Pop. "He found it in Wooster's room, you say?"

"Concealed beneath his underwear."

Pop Bassett uttered a sound like the wind going out of a dying duck.

"How right you were, Roderick! You said his motive in coming here was to steal this. But how he got into the collection room I cannot understand."

"These fellows have their methods."

"Seems to be a great demand for that thing," said Plank. "There was a young slab of damnation with a criminal face round at my place only yesterday trying to sell it to me."

"Wooster!"

"No, it wasn't Wooster. My fellow's name was Alpine Joe."

"Wooster would naturally adopt a pseudonym."

"I suppose he would. I never thought of that."

"Well, after this—" said Pop Bassett.

"Yes, after this," said Spode, "you're certainly not going

to marry the man, Madeline. He's worse than Fink-Nottle."

"Who's Fink-Nottle?" asked Plank.

"The one who eloped with Stoker," said Pop.

"Who's Stoker?" asked Plank. I don't think I've ever came across a fellow with a greater thirst for information.

"The cook."

"Ah yes. I remember you telling me. Knew what he was doing, that chap. I'm strongly opposed to anyone marrying anybody, but if you're going to marry someone, you unquestionably save something from the wreck by marrying a woman who knows what to do with a joint of beef. There was a fellow I knew in the Federated Malay States who——"

It would probably have been a diverting anecdote, but Spode didn't let him get on with it any further. Addressing Madeline, he said: "What you're going to do is marry me, and I don't want any argument. How about it, Madeline?"

"Yes, Roderick. I will be your wife."

Spode uttered a whoop which made my nose tickle worse than ever.

"That's the stuff! That's how I like to hear you talk! Come on out into the garden. I have much to say to you."

I imagine that at this juncture he must have folded her in his embrace and hustled her out, for I heard the door close. And as it did so Pop Bassett uttered a whoop somewhat similar in its intensity to the one that had proceeded from the Spode lips. He was patently boomps-a-daisy, and one could readily understand why. A father whose daughter, after nearly marrying Gussie Fink-Nottle and then nearly marrying me, sees the light and hooks on to a prosperous member of the British aristocracy is entitled to rejoice. I didn't like Spode and would have been glad at any time to see a Peruvian matron spike him in the leg with her dagger, but there was no denying that he was hot stuff matrimonially.

[207]

"Lady Sidcup!" said Pop, rolling the words round his tongue like vintage port.

"Who's Lady Sidcup?" asked Plank, anxious, as always, to keep abreast.

"My daughter will shortly be. One of the oldest titles in England. That was Lord Sidcup who has just left us."

"I thought his name was Roderick."

"His Christian name is Roderick."

"Ah!" said Plank. "Now I've got it. Now I have the whole picture. Your daughter was to have married someone called Fink-Nottle?"

"Yes."

"Then she was to have married this chap Wooster or Alpine Joe, as the case may be?"

"Yes."

"And now she's going to marry Lord Sidcup?"

"Yes."

"Clear as crystal," said Plank. "I knew I should get it threshed out in time. Simply a matter of concentration and elimination. You approve of this marriage? As far," he added, "as one can approve of any marriage?"

"I most certainly do."

"Then I think this calls for another whiskey-and-soda."

"I will join you," said Pop Bassett.

It was at this point, unable to hold it back any longer, that I sneezed.

"I knew there was something behind that sofa," said Plank, rounding it and subjecting me to the sort of look he had once given native chiefs who couldn't grasp the rules of Rugby football. "Odd sounds came from that direction. Good God, it's Alpine Joe."

"It's Wooster!"

"Who's Wooster? Oh, you told me, didn't you? What steps do you propose to take?"

"I have rung for Butterfield."

"Who's Butterfield?"

"My butler."

"What do you want a butler for?"

"To tell him to bring Oates."

"Who's Oates?"

"Our local policeman. He is having a glass of whiskey in the kitchen."

"Whiskey!" said Plank thoughtfully, and, as if reminded of something, went to the side table.

The door opened.

"Oh, Butterfield, will you tell Oates to come here."

"Very good, Sir Watkyn."

"Bit out of condition, that chap," said Plank, eyeing Butterfield's retreating back. "Wants a few games of Rugger to put him in shape. What are you going to do about this Alpine Joe fellow? You going to charge him?"

"I certainly am. No doubt he assumed that I would shrink from causing a scandal, but he was wrong. I shall let the law take its course."

"Quite right. Soak him to the utmost limit. You're a Justice of the Peace, aren't you?"

"I am, and intend to give him twenty-eight days in the second division."

"Or sixty? Nice round number, sixty. You couldn't make it six months, I suppose?"

"I fear not."

"No, I imagine you have a regular tariff. Ah, well, twenty-eight days is better than nothing."

"Police Constable Oates," said Butterfield in the doorway.

CHAPTER
TWENTY-FOUR

I DON'T know why it is, but there's something about being hauled off to a police bin that makes you feel a bit silly. At least, that's how it always affects me. I mean, there you are, you and the arm of the law, toddling along side by side, and you feel that in a sense he's your host and you ought to show an interest and try to draw him out. But it's so difficult to hit on anything in the nature of an exchange of ideas, and conversation never really flows. I remember at my private school, the one I won a prize for Scripture Knowledge at, the Rev. Aubrey Upjohn, the top brass, used to take us one by one for an educational walk on Sunday afternoons, and I always found it hard to sparkle when my turn came to step out at his side. It was the same on this occasion, when I accompanied Constable Oates to the village coop. It's no good my pretending the thing went with a swing, because it didn't.

Probably if I'd been one of the topnotchers, about to do a ten-year stretch for burglary or arson or what not, it would have been different, but I was only one of the small fry who get twenty-eight days in the second division, and I couldn't help thinking the officer was looking down on me. Not actually sneering, perhaps, but aloof in his manner, as if feeling I wasn't much for a cop to get his teeth into.

And, of course, there was another thing. Speaking of my earlier visit to Totleigh Towers, I mentioned that when Pop Bassett immured me in my room, he stationed the local police force on the lawn below to see that I didn't nip out of the window. That local police force was this same Oates, and as it was raining like the dickens at the time, no doubt the episode had rankled. Only a very sunny constable can look with an indulgent eye on the fellow responsible for his getting the nastiest cold in the head of his career.

At any rate, he showed himself now a man of few words, though good at locking people up in cells. There was only one at the Totleigh-in-the-Wold emporium, and I had it all to myself, a cozy little apartment with a window, not barred but too small to get out of, a grille in the door, a plank bed, and that rather powerful aroma of drunks and disorderlies which you always find in these homes from home. Whether it was superior or inferior to the one they had given me at Bosher Street, I was unable to decide. Not much in it either way, it seemed to me.

To say that when I turned in on the plank bed I fell into a dreamless sleep would be deceiving my public. I passed a somewhat restless night. I could have sworn, indeed, that I didn't drop off at all, but I suppose I must have done, because the next thing I knew sunlight was coming through the window and mine host was bringing me breakfast.

I got outside it with an appetite unusual with me at such an early hour, and at the conclusion of the meal I fished out an old envelope and did what I have sometimes done before when the bludgeonings of Fate were up and about to any extent—viz., make a list of Credits and Debits, as I believe Robinson Crusoe used to. The idea being to see whether I was ahead of or behind the game at moment of going to press.

The final score worked out as follows:

CREDIT	DEBIT
Not at all a bad breakfast, that. Coffee quite good. I was surprised.	Don't always be thinking of your stomach, you jailbird.
Who's a jailbird?	You're a jailbird.
Well, yes, I suppose I am, if you care to put it that way. But I am innocent. My hands are clean.	More than your face is.
Not looking my best, what?	You look like something the cat brought in.
A bath will put that right.	And you'll get one in prison.
You really think it'll come to that?	Well, you heard what Pop Bassett said.
I wonder what it's like, doing twenty-eight days? Hitherto, I've always just come for the night.	You'll hate it. It'll bore you stiff.
I don't know so much. They give you a cake of soap and a hymnbook, don't they?	What's the good of a cake of soap and a hymnbook?

[212]

I'll be able to whack up some sort of
    indoor game with them. And don't
    forget that I've not got to marry
    Madeline Bassett. Let's hear what
    you have to say to that.

And the Debit account didn't utter. I had baffled it.

Yes, I felt, as I hunted around in case there might be a
crumb of bread which I had overlooked, that amply com-
pensated me for the vicissitudes I was undergoing. And I
had been musing along these lines for a while, getting more
and more reconciled to my lot, when a silvery voice spoke,
making me jump like a startled grasshopper. I couldn't think
where it was coming from at first and speculated for a moment on the possibility of it being my guardian angel,
though I had always thought of him, I don't know why, as
being of the male sex. Then I saw something not unlike a
human face at the grille, and a closer inspection told me
that it was Stiffy.

I Hullo-there-ed cordially and expressed some surprise at
finding her on the premises.

"I wouldn't have thought Oates would have let you in.
It isn't Visitors Day, is it?"

She explained that the zealous officer had gone up to the
house to see her Uncle Watkyn and that she had sneaked in
when he had legged it.

"Oh, Bertie," she said, "I wish I could slip you in a file."

"What would I do with a file?"

"Saw through the bars, of course, ass."

"There aren't any bars."

"Oh, aren't there? That's a difficulty. We'll have to let
it go, then. Have you had breakfast?"

"Just finished."

"Was it all right?"

"Fairly toothsome."

"I'm glad to hear that, because I'm weighed down with remorse."

"You are? Why?"

"Use the loaf. If I hadn't pinched that statuette thing, none of this would have happened."

"Oh, I wouldn't worry."

"But I do worry. Shall I tell Uncle Watkyn that you're innocent, because I was the guilty party? You ought to have your name cleared."

I put the bee on this suggestion with the greatest promptitude.

"Certainly not. Don't dream of it."

"But don't you want your name cleared?"

"Not at the expense of you taking the rap."

"Uncle Watkyn wouldn't send me to chokey."

"I dare say not, but Stinker would learn all and would be shocked to the core."

"Coo! I didn't think of that."

"Think of it now. He wouldn't be able to help asking himself if it was a prudent move for a vicar to link his lot with yours. Doubts, that's what he'd have, and qualms. It isn't as if you were going to be a gangster's moll. The gangster would be all for you swiping everything in sight and would encourage you with word and gesture, but it's different with Stinker. When he marries you, he'll want you to take charge of the parish funds. Apprise him of the facts, and he won't have an easy moment."

"I see what you mean. Yes, you have a point there."

"Picture his jumpiness if he found you near the Sunday offertory bag. No, secrecy and silence is the only course."

She sighed a bit, as if her conscience was troubling her, but she saw the force of my reasoning.

"I suppose you're right, but I do hate the idea of you doing time."

"There are compensations."

"Such as?"

"I am saved from the scaffold."

"The —? Oh, I see what you mean. You get out of marrying Madeline."

"Exactly, and, as I remember telling you once, I am implying nothing derogatory to Madeline when I say that the thought of being united to her in bonds of holy wedlock was one that gave your old friend shivers down the spine. The fact is in no way to her discredit. I should feel just the same about marrying many of the world's noblest women. There are certain females whom one respects, admires, reveres, but only from a distance, and it is to this group that Madeline belongs."

And I was about to develop this theme, with possibly a reference to those folk songs, when a gruff voice interrupted our tête-à-tête, if you can call a thing a tête-à-tête when the two of you are on opposite sides of an iron grille. It was Constable Oates, returned from his excursion. Stiffy's presence displeased him, and he spoke austerely.

"What's all this?" he demanded.

"What's all what?" riposted Stiffy with spirit, and I remember thinking that she rather had him there.

"It's against regulations to talk to the prisoner, miss."

"Oates," said Stiffy, "you're an ass."

This was profoundly true, but it seemed to annoy the officer. He resented the charge, and said so, and Stiffy said she didn't want any backchat from him.

"You road-company rozzers make me sick. I was only trying to cheer him up."

It seemed to me that the officer gave a bitter snort, and a moment later he revealed why he had done so.

"It's me that wants cheering up," he said morosely. "I've just seen Sir Watkyn, and he says he isn't pressing the charge."

"What!" I cried.

"What!" yipped Stiffy.

"That's what," said the constable, and you could see that while there was sunshine above, there was none in his heart. I could sympathize with him, of course. Naturally nothing makes a member of the force sicker than to have a criminal get away from him. He was in rather the same position as some crocodile on the Zambesi or some puma in Brazil would have been if it had earmarked Plank for its lunch and seen him skin up a high tree.

"Shackling the police, that's what I call it," he said, and I think he spat on the floor. I couldn't see him, of course, but I was aware of a spitlike sound.

Stiffy whooped, well pleased, and I whooped myself, if I remember correctly. For all the bold front I had been putting up, I had never in my heart really liked the idea of rotting for twenty-eight days in a dungeon cell. Prison is all right for a night, but you don't want to go overdoing the thing.

"Then what are we waiting for?" said Stiffy. "Get a move on, officer. Fling wide those gates."

Oates flung them, not attempting to conceal his chagrin and disappointment, and I passed with Stiffy into the great world outside the prison walls.

"Goodbye, Oates," I said as we left, for one always likes to do the courteous thing. "It's been nice meeting you. How are Mrs. Oates and the little ones?"

His only reply was a sound like a hippopotamus taking

its foot out of the mud on a riverbank, and I saw Stiffy frown, as though his manner offended her.

"You know," she said as we reached the open spaces, "we really ought to do something about Oates, something that would teach him that we're not put into this world for pleasure alone. I can't suggest what offhand, but if we put our heads together, we could think of something. You ought to stay on, Bertie, and help me bring his ginger hairs in sorrow to the grave."

I raised an eyebrow.

"As the guest of your Uncle Watkyn?"

"You could muck in with Harold. There's a spare room at that cottage place of his."

"Sorry, no."

"You won't stay on?"

"I will not. I intend to put as many miles as possible in as short a time as possible between Totleigh-in-the-Wold and myself. And it's no good your using that expression 'lily-livered poltroon,' because I am adamant."

She made what I believe is called a *moue*. It's done by pushing the lips out and drawing them in again.

"I thought it wouldn't be any use asking you. No spirit, that's your trouble; no enterprise. I'll have to get Harold to do it."

And as I stood shuddering at the picture her words conjured up, she pushed off, exhibiting dudgeon. And I was still speculating as to what tureen of soup she was planning to land the sainted Pinker in and hoping that he would have enough sense to stay out of it, when Jeeves drove up in the car, a welcome sight.

"Good morning, sir," he said. "I trust you slept well."

"Fitfully, Jeeves. Those plank beds are not easy on the fleshy parts."

[217]

"So I would be disposed to imagine, sir. And your disturbed night has left you ruffled, I am sorry to see. You are far from *soigné.*"

I could, I suppose, have said something about "Way down upon the *soigné* river," but I didn't. My mind was occupied with deeper thoughts. I was in pensive mood.

"You know, Jeeves," I said, "one lives and learns."

"Sir?"

"I mean, this episode has been a bit of an eye-opener to me. It has taught me a lesson. I see now what a mistake one makes in labeling someone as a ruddy Gawd-help-us just because he normally behaves like a ruddy Gawd-help-us. Look closely, and we find humanity in the unlikeliest places."

"A broad-minded view, sir."

"Take this Sir W. Bassett. In my haste, I have always penciled him in as a hellhound without a single redeeming quality. But what do I find? He has this softer side to him. Having got Bertram out on a limb, he does not, as one would have expected, proceed to saw it off but tempers justice with mercy, declining to press the charge. It has touched me a good deal to discover that under that forbidding exterior there lies a heart of gold. Why are you looking like a stuffed frog, Jeeves? Don't you agree with me?"

"Not altogether, sir, when you attribute Sir Watkyn's leniency to sheer goodness of heart. There were inducements."

"I don't dig you, Jeeves."

"I made it a condition that you be set at liberty, sir."

My inability to dig him became intensified. He seemed to me to be talking through the back of his neck, the last thing you desire in a personal attendant.

"How do you mean, condition? Condition of what?"

[218]

"Of my entering his employment, sir. I should mention that during my visit to Brinkley Court Sir Watkyn very kindly expressed appreciation of the manner in which I performed my duties and made me an offer to leave your service and enter his. This offer, conditional upon your release, I have accepted."

The police station at Totleigh-in-the-Wold is situated in the main street of that village, and from where we were standing I had a view of the establishments of a butcher, a baker, a grocer, and a publican licensed to sell tobacco, ales, and spirits. And as I heard these words, this butcher, this baker, this grocer, and this publican seemed to pirouette before my eyes as if afflicted with St. Vitus's dance.

"You're leaving me?" I gasped, scarcely able to b. my e.

The corner of his mouth twitched. He seemed to be about to smile but of course thought better of it.

"Only temporarily, sir."

Again I was unable to dig him.

"Temporarily?"

"I think it more than possible that after perhaps a week or so differences will arise between Sir Watkyn and myself, compelling me to resign my position. In that event, if you are not already suited, sir, I shall be most happy to return to your employment."

I saw all. It was a ruse, and by no means the worst of them. His brain enlarged by constant helpings of fish, he had seen the way and found a formula acceptable to all parties. The mists cleared from before my eyes, and the butcher, the baker, the grocer, and the publican licensed to sell tobacco, ales, and spirits switched back again to what is called the status quo.

A rush of emotion filled me.

"Jeeves," I said, and if my voice shook, what of it? We

[219]

Woosters are but human. "You stand alone. Others abide our question, but you don't, as the fellow said. I wish there was something I could do to repay you."

He coughed that sheeplike cough of his.

"There does chance to be a favor it is within your power to bestow, sir."

"Name it, Jeeves. Ask of me what you will, even unto half my kingdom."

"If you could see your way to abandoning your Alpine hat, sir."

I ought to have seen it coming. That cough should have told me. But I hadn't, and the shock was severe. I don't mind admitting that for an instant I reeled.

"You would go as far as that?" I said, chewing the lower lip.

"It was merely a suggestion, sir."

I took the hat off and gazed at it. The morning sunlight played on it, and it had never looked so blue, its feather so pink.

"I suppose you know you're breaking my heart?"

"I am sorry, sir."

I sighed. But, as I have said, the Woosters can take it.

"Very well, Jeeves. So be it."

I gave him the hat. It made me feel like a father reluctantly throwing his child from the sledge to divert the attention of the pursuing wolf pack, as I believe happens all the time in Russia in the winter months, but what would you?

"You propose to burn this Alpine hat, Jeeves?"

"No, sir. To present it to Mr. Butterfield. He thinks it will be of assistance to him in his courtship."

"His what?"

"Mr. Butterfield is courting a widowed lady in the village, sir."

This surprised me.

"But surely he was a hundred and four last birthday?"

"He is well stricken in years, yes, sir, but nevertheless—"

"There's life in the old dog yet?"

"Precisely, sir."

My heart melted. I ceased to think of self. It had just oc-curred to me that in the circumstances I would be unable to conclude my visit by tipping Butterfield. The hat would fill that gap.

"All right, Jeeves, give him the lid, and heaven speed his wooing. You might tell him that from me."

"I will make a point of doing so. Thank you very much, sir."

"Not at all, Jeeves."